SUSAN YAWN TANNER

Callahan Goes Rodeo

Secret Staircase Books

Cat Callahan Mysteries
by Rebecca Barrett and Susan Yawn Tanner

Callahan on the Case
Callahan and the Horses of Hope
Callahan's Savannah Caper
Callahan Goes Rodeo
Callahan's Christmas Feast (short story)
A Callahan Christmas (short story)

Susan Yawn Tanner

Callahan Goes Rodeo

Cat Callahan Mysteries, Book 4

Callahan Goes Rodeo
Published by Secret Staircase Books, an imprint of
Columbine Publishing Group LLC
PO Box 416, Angel Fire, NM 87710

Book layout and design by Secret Staircase Books
Illustrations by Becky's Graphic Design, Michael Turner,
Michael Gray, Kalinin Dmitrii

First e-book edition: April, 2024
First paperback edition: April, 2024
An earlier version of this story was published in 2018
as *Turning For Trouble*

Publisher's Cataloging-in-Publication Data

Tanner, Susan Yawn
Callahan Goes Rodeo / by Susan Yawn Tanner.
p. cm.
ISBN 978-1649141750 (paperback)
ISBN 978-1649141767 (e-book)

1. Cat Callahan (Fictitious character)—Fiction. 2. Southern
Mysteries—Fiction. 3. Amateur sleuths—Fiction. I. Title

Cat Callahan Mystery Series, Book 4.
Tanner, Susan Yawn, Cat Callahan Mysteries.

BISAC : FICTION / Mystery.

813/.54

*To the fabulous four…Sybil, Lenora, Janice, Debbie…
friends, family, faithful, forever.*

Acknowledgements

Many talented writers have given a helping hand in my own journey…Carolyn Haines and Rebecca Barrett, who always believed in me, cj petterson who supports me publicly and unfailingly, and C. Terry Cline and Judith Richards who encouraged me and who will be forever missed.

Chapter 1

No one would ever call me a romantic sort of cat. Not that I haven't enjoyed my fair share of opportunities. Maybe even more than my fair share. But, me and Dax, we're ramblin' sorts, always moving on, leaving the past behind. Not that I've seen Dax pay much attention to any of the female humans, although a good number have given him a second look, and maybe a third. He seems content with his rag-tag books and the old movie reels on his cell phone, which is forever in need of charging.

One of those videos is how he tagged me with the name Callahan. The guy on the screen is Detective Callahan to the perps ... that's bad guy in cop jargon ... but the other officers call him Dirty Harry.

Guess I'm lucky Dax picked Callahan for my moniker. Cats are not dirty. Even under the worst of circumstances.

Romance aside, wedding or not, no one could grumble about this sunny October day, not cold but cool enough for comfort. It's almost as perfect as the bride. Not that Dax or I are officially invited to the festivities. Dax has stayed far away from the gathered crowd as is his tendency. Me? I'm on the prowl for chow. There's almost always a human or two willing to share.

We haven't moved far from our last job … Dax as hired hand on this working cattle ranch, me as helping hand … er … paw! It doesn't look big or fancy but it's orderly, and I think it must do okay. They have enough money to pay Dax, and both of us eat well, which is my personal measure of success.

The everlasting heat and humidity of summer in the South have been brushed aside by the dry, crisp breezes of an early fall just in time for this shindig. And, now, with the afternoon fading to evening, the fairy lights twinkle to life in the soft twilight. I'm not sure what fairies are, but the lights hung out for them aren't bad at all.

And there! The deed is done. The knot is tied. Let the party begin! I intend to celebrate in my own way. While the humans spin themselves around a dance floor built only for that reason, I'll visit the food stations to sample the wares. I'll skip the green stuff, but I see beef on a stick and chicken in some kind of wrapper. Too bad I don't have a way to carry something back to Dax. But that's on him. He could have joined me.

* * *

Malone Summers was more than happy for the bride and groom. Though she didn't see her old friend as much as they both wished, they'd remained good friends through the years. Heaven knew Kelli deserved this second opportunity at a happy marriage. Malone didn't much believe in second chances where love was concerned, but she wished the best for Kelli. The bride was radiant, looking half her age, and twirling in the arms of her handsome groom as if she were a teenager.

Malone planned to slip into the crowd well before the dance floor was opened up to the wedding guests. She had no intention of dancing though she had loved it once, probably still did, truth be told, but it wasn't a thing she indulged in anymore. There were many things she no longer allowed herself. Life's lessons had been hard, but she'd learned them well.

Smiling at the wedding couple's happiness, she turned and walked straight into a broad chest and strong hands that caught her shoulders ever so lightly. Her glance registered a swift impression of an expertly tailored suit in the same moment she caught the light scent of aftershave mixed with pure masculinity. But when she looked up into eyes so pale a grey as to be silver when the light caught them just right, her heart dropped in her chest. She would, she had no doubt, remember those eyes for all of her years. And she had long ago accepted the fact.

"Excuse me," she murmured, stepping back and out of the light grip of those hands before he recognized her, if he even would.

She felt his gaze on her back as she walked away, but she didn't turn around.

* * *

Day was barely breaking as Malone put a halter on Jaz and led the big sorrel mare out of the barn and into the morning, toward the truck and trailer. It was still early, still chilly, that peaceful time of day she enjoyed most when the sun was just barely over the horizon.

Normally, she would have lingered, at least for a little a while. Kelli's ranch, with her barn filled with talented horses, was one of her favorite places to visit. Today, however, Malone wanted to be gone before any of the other wedding guests roused themselves. Not even to herself would she admit there was only one person she hoped to avoid. With any luck at all, Cade Delaney was sleeping off a good time.

Malone smiled at the sight of Kelli propped against the hood of her truck, two steaming mugs in her hands and a gray cat twining around her dusty boots. At her approach, Kelli pushed away from the truck and handed her one of the mugs.

"What in the world is the bride doing up at this hour?" Malone eyed Kelli over an appreciative sip of coffee that tasted every bit as heavenly as it smelled.

Kelli chuckled. "I couldn't keep my eyes from opening. I'll nap on the plane."

"I can't believe you're actually taking time for a honeymoon."

"I can't either, really. I've always wanted to see Wales but never dreamed I would. Frank smooth-talked me into it."

"Good for Frank. And good for you for finding a way to trust again."

Kelli nodded. She would know where Malone's thoughts had gone. "It wasn't easy, but if I can, you can."

"I'd have to want to," Malone said lightly, "and I don't." To take any sting out of her response, she added with real honesty, "I'm too happy with my life now—finally—to risk changing anything."

As if on cue, the door to the guest cabin closest to them opened, and Malone caught a glimpse of Cade in her peripheral vision as he stepped through with a small tote in hand. Damn. And he naturally turned toward his hostess and Malone. Double damn.

A beautiful dog, Australian Shepherd—from the coat and color—walked beside him. She automatically glanced at the gray cat, but he showed no sign of interest, much less alarm.

"Kelli. Malone." Cade greeted them both in the same pleasant tone.

Kelli's eyes widened. "You two know each other? But, of course, I forget, you both make your living in rodeo."

Before Malone could speak, before she could casually agree as she intended, Cade said, "We knew each other before that." His gaze caught on Malone's. "Long before."

Mercifully that silver gaze moved on to Jaz standing quietly on her lead line. "Nice mare."

Malone let a little of the tension ease from her shoulders. "I got her last summer. She's been pulling some nice checks at the pay window since January when I started hauling her in earnest. She's been at the top of my string the last couple of months. I'm lucky to have her."

"She's lucky to have *you*," Kelli returned the compliment as she glanced at Cade again.

The expression on Kelli's face telegraphed her curiosity at the earlier nuances of Malone's exchange with Cade, but to Malone's relief she asked no questions. Instead, she said, "I've watched your success, the videos you've posted and some televised rodeos. I can tell she loves her job as much as you do."

"Thank you. She's a really nice gal." Feeling antsy under Cade's steady regard, Malone handed Kelli the empty mug. "I appreciate the coffee, and the wedding was lovely. I'm going to get my horses loaded and head out. I've got a full week ahead of me."

"Both Frank and I were happy that you could be here. I put a thermos of coffee in the front of your truck when I saw you throw your bag in the back and head for the barn, but we'd love for you to have brunch before you leave. Frank was already poking around in the kitchen when I stepped out. He's planning to feed anyone who is awake enough to eat."

No way was Malone spending the next couple of hours with Cade watching her. She declined with a smile and a word of thanks and led Jaz around to the side of the trailer. To her consternation, Cade and his dog followed. Without asking, Cade lowered the loading ramp with quiet efficiency.

Not wanting to sound as ungrateful as she felt, she murmured thanks she didn't feel. She'd been taking care of herself for a long time, and she didn't plan for that to ever change.

"Where are you headed?"

Cade's question surprised her, not the words, but the fact that he'd asked, that he'd bother to ask. And she didn't want to tell him, but he'd find out anyway if he really wanted to know.

"LaGrange."

His brows lifted at that. "Opposite direction of Oklahoma." She knew the comment wasn't as casual as it seemed. LaGrange had once been home to both of them, but he'd most likely know her mother had died and her father had remarried, sold their property there, and moved out of state. She wasn't about to ask how he knew she was entered in Oklahoma City in little more than a week. Cade might be the new Director of Operations for Twin Circuit Rodeos, but exactly what competitor was entered and where wasn't something anyone would expect him to be aware of. In the end, she simply answered his question as if there were no unhappy history between them.

"Granddad left me his place. I suspect there are some things of his I'll want to keep so I need a day or two to sort through them before I call a real estate agent to list it."

"I heard you'd lost him." All of the edge had left his expression and his voice, or maybe she'd only imagined his tension because *she* felt it. "I know that hurt."

"It did, yes." She didn't need to ask how he'd known. Her granddad's place bordered the Delaney property, and Cade and his family were probably still very close. He hadn't disappointed, hadn't shamed his parents as she had hers.

For the next few minutes, she focused on loading and securing each of her horses in turn, but she knew Cade was still there, still watching, and wasn't the least surprised when he moved in to help her raise and secure the ramp.

She turned to face him, feeling unexpectedly awkward. "Thanks for the help. I'll see you down the road, I guess."

"Yes." That was all he said, and she couldn't read a thing in his expression. Or maybe she just didn't want to.

He stepped back as she climbed up into the cab of her truck and she pulled away.

* * *

Interesting thing about humans, they don't always say in words what's communicated in their eyes and their expressions. While these two dance around the looks they're giving each other, I'll take a turn around the large truck and trailer to ensure everything's in good repair and safe for the long haul. That's cowhand speak for the lengthy trip ahead. Not that I consider myself a cowhand, but I've managed to pick up some of the lingo.

I've learned through my interaction with what was once called the weaker of the human sexes that they're as capable and competent as any of the men, maybe more so. Still, there's a point of chivalry in any real male that requires this extra vigilance on their behalf. I find I'm not alone in that as I notice Cade eyeing the tires of her rig to be sure they're up to the trip.

All of the various side compartments, and there are several, seem securely closed.

But as I turn the corner to check out the opposite side, an inch or two of faded denim, along with worn leather boots, disappear beneath a long, narrow access that is slowly lowered. Malone is about to have a stowaway, and I can see very little but a pair of eyes staring back at me! Those eyes are dulled by some emotion, at best despair, at worst something more ominous. I can't tell if this is friend or foe and cannot leave Malone to be taken unaware somewhere down the road, maybe an isolated rest stop. I'd best give her a heads up.

I realize I'm too late for that when I hear the truck engine start with a growl. There's not much time to react. All I can do is leap forward and hope that the opening of the compartment is wide enough for me to slip through and that the somber-eyed human doesn't grasp my plan in time to lower the metal hatch even more.

I'm in, and just in the nick of time, as the truck and trailer move forward. The human with me gasps as the hatch slams shut, and we both realize we have a problem.

Well, this wasn't my plan for the day, but there's not much help for it now. My night vision kicks in, and I study the human who stares back at me with considerable dismay.

Chapter 2

Malone pulled into the drive, cut the engine, and simply sat at the wheel of her truck, drinking in the remembered beauty of the place with its weathered yet stout fencing and sturdy outbuildings. The house itself was by no means grand, but the wraparound porch was homey and welcoming. It welcomed her as it always had.

The three-hour drive to the property her grandparents had left her had been uneventful, giving her plenty of time to think, to wonder if she were making the right choice in even considering calling an agent.

This had once been more home to her than the house and property her parents had owned. She knew she'd disappointed them, embarrassed them. She wondered if they'd ever realized they'd done the same to her. Her father's distant reserve, never speaking or smiling when her friends came around; her mother's relentless fault-finding, regardless of who was within hearing. The years and miles had taught her that only they were to blame for their discontent, but there'd been a time she'd blamed first herself, then each of them for the other's miserable outlook. She knew better now, but it had been a lesson only time and experience could teach.

As a child, she'd fled their unhappiness every chance she could. She'd been seven the first year she'd been allowed to stay with her grandparents for the three blissful months of school vacation. Twelve-year-old Cade had taught her to ride fearlessly. Summer after summer, her granddad had permitted her to tag along with Cade's family—friends as well as neighbors—to local rodeos. Cade had shared his rope horse with her, helped her train him for barrels, paid her entry fee from time to time with cash hard-earned at summer jobs. If she closed her eyes, she could see him still, stepping into the alleyway at the end of a run, catching her rein, his face beaming with pride. And if she looked toward the rolling hills just to the north, she had no doubt she'd see a younger Cade letting his horse pick his way carefully across the uneven ground toward her with the summer sun beating down.

But that had been a lifetime ago and time moved on.

Sighing, she released her seatbelt and stepped down into the sunlit morning. The first order of business was to get the horses where they could move about in safety, where they could roll and stretch with a playful buck or two.

Her phone was ringing as she stepped to the ground but stopped before she could fish it from the back pocket of her jeans. Not recognizing the number, she turned toward the rear of the trailer only to have the same number ringing in again. It could be a new client with a horse rodeo-ready but still in need of someone to do the hard part of hauling and seasoning until the animal was rock-solid. The fact that she was currently booked never made her ignore courtesy. And she had never become so complacent as to lose sight of the truth that the living she made was as much on her reputation and interaction with her clients as on her riding skills and tireless work.

She answered as she always did, "This is Malone."

"Put Cowboy on the phone."

The voice was unfamiliar and rude, so rude that she tempered her own tone to cool restraint.

"You have the wrong number."

"No, you have the wrong answer. We know where LaMonte goes to ground."

The use of the word *We* rather than *I* sent a small prickle through her veins. She leaned against the side of the truck wondering what trouble Tyge had gotten himself into this time. "I haven't seen Tyge in over a year. I don't know where you got my number, but I'd like for you to lose it."

"You tell Cowboy he can't hide behind a woman's skirts forever. It might take us a while, but we'll catch up with you. And him."

Again, *us* not *me*. Without answering, Malone disconnected the call, feeling that old flare of tension. She pushed it aside, gratified to realize that it took far less effort these days. Tyge, the rough stock rider she'd left home with at seventeen, had lived with, loved with, but never married, had been in some kind of trouble off and on for years. He always found a way to finagle himself out of the repercussions.

Resolutely, she turned her mind to making the horses comfortable and happy before going inside to see what kind of mess might await her. The house had remained vacant since her grandfather's death. Malone paid a local service to walk through it once a week to open windows and air it out for a few hours, to make certain appliances were running, doors remained locked, and windows unbroken. Mostly Malone needed to ensure no vagrants took up residence until she felt herself capable of making a decision about the house, the property. She didn't know for sure if she'd reached that point, but it was past time to do something.

For a moment, she leaned against the fence rail, watching as Jaz explored the grassy paddock. She sent a check each month to her grandfather's closest neighbor and best friend. He'd engaged a local handyman to bush hog the fenced areas around the barn and house on a regular basis. Her gaze lifted to the empty slope of the hills. The cows had been sold at her request. Those hills would soon be overtaken by scrub trees. Or housing projects. The thought depressed her and she turned resolutely to get fresh water to the horses.

As she neared the truck and trailer, the sound of a cat yowling startled her. Glancing around, she saw nothing, but the closer she came to the trailer the louder the sound.

* * *

Well, this is a pickle. These side compartments open easily enough from the outside but—not being designed for occupancy whether by human or cat—have no handles on the inside. I feel a sense of desperation growing in the young female beside me as she runs her hands along the crevices.

I've at least had time to realize that this young miss, desperate though she is at the moment, is no threat to Malone. I'm savvy enough to know that strong fright can make the actions of any human unpredictable, but I don't detect any meanness in the girl. I allowed her to pull me onto her lap for the ride. It gave her comfort to hold another living creature, I think. And who wouldn't be comforted by me? It also gave me a warmer, softer ride than the unyielding metal of the compartment floor. So, selfish on my part, but that's no crime. Two birds, one stone, I say.

Could be the girl thought to leave the door unlatched so that it would give to pressure upon arrival at our destination, where ever that may be. Or could be she didn't think at all in her plan for escape and, I haven't a doubt, an escape it was. But from whom or what, I've no idea. Yet. She's not a talkative thing for certain. Other than a whispered, "Oh no!" she hasn't spoken since I leapt into the hatch with her.

Time for me to alert Malone to our presence, as I can't be sure she'll discover us soon enough for my comfort. I've no idea how the girl will react for she clearly doesn't want her existence known.

* * *

Malone stopped at the trailer and listened, but the cat had stopped yowling. She reached into the trailer compartment for a water bucket and the sound came again, louder and closer, with an echoing quality. She couldn't imagine how a cat came to be trapped in her trailer, but it was there somewhere, and close. Malone reached cautiously for the handle on the next compartment and lifted the door, stepping to one side as she did. She had no desire for a frightened cat to take a flying leap toward her face.

But, no, a plush, gray cat sat quietly watching as she raised the door. And, there, pressed into the shadows of a corner, a young woman—no, nowhere near a woman, not more than a school girl—stared back at her.

"You'll need to climb out now."

"Don't tell them where I am." The voice held both fear and defiance.

"Climb out," Malone repeated, more calmly than she felt, not ready to admit she was alone on the property, not yet certain the girl was alone in there. She had her small Smith & Wesson Shield in the truck, but it wasn't much use to her from here.

The cat leapt out first and Malone gave a groan as she caught full sight of him. "Good grief! You're Dax's cat!" There was no mistaking that golden gaze. "At least I think that's what Kelli called him. Dax. What in the world were you doing in there?"

The girl emerged more slowly and Malone took in the faded jeans and nondescript tee shirt. Green-gold eyes with heavy lashes brushed fair skin as she blinked at the bright sunshine. Hair pulled up under a plain red ball cap, the wisps that escaped dark, almost black, even in the daylight. Any lingering uneasiness at discovering a stowaway yielded to dismay when the morning rays revealed the dark bruise on one cheek.

Malone caught her breath audibly but said nothing for a moment, then, softly, "You're hurt."

The girl shrugged without responding. Her gaze was steady and guarded.

Malone's sweeping glance caught a glimpse of another bruise just below the sleeve of her tee shirt. Keeping her tone even, she asked, "Do you need medical attention?"

At the suggestion, something flashed deep within her eyes. "No." She shifted a tiny step back. "I just needed a ride, just needed to get away."

Realizing the girl was on the point of flight, Malone gestured around her at the empty property with its aura of abandonment. "You're very much *away* here. Who are you running from?"

"It doesn't matter. We've got to be far enough away from Louisiana that surely it doesn't matter. What state is this?"

"Georgia." Then the girl's words caught up with Malone. "What? Wait! Are you saying you got on this trailer in Louisiana? At the rodeo in Lake Charles?" That had been Malone's last stop, her last run, before arriving at Kelli's.

At the girl's nod, Malone blew out a breath. She had questions. Too many. And most weren't going to get answered any time soon if that closed expression was any indication. "Okay, this can wait. I've got to get my mare some water then we'll go inside and talk. And find something for you to eat."

"No, ma'am, I'll just be on my way."

Callahan growled low in his throat at the girl's words.

Malone studied her in consternation. The girl was an unknown entity with a past that could hold anything, any amount of trouble that Malone didn't need. But, to just let her wander away with a destination and a fate unknown was beyond Malone. "Where are you headed?"

"Anywhere." The girl reached back and pulled a duffle bag from the trailer compartment. "Someplace I can get a job."

She didn't look old enough, Malone thought and almost asked, then realized the girl would only lie if she were as young as Malone suspected. Clearly, she had no one to help her, at least no one she trusted. Malone had stopped acting on impulse long ago. At least she thought she'd stopped until she opened her mouth and said, "I could use a hand here, at least for a couple of days."

"Here?" The girl looked suspicious. "Doing what?"

Exasperated with herself at making the offer and at the girl's suspicions, Malone asked with a trace of asperity, "Does it really matter? Work is work. Money is money. Food and a roof over your head are just that."

For the first time, a glimmer of a smile touched the girl's face. "No, ma'am, I don't suppose it does matter."

Malone took a deep breath, wondering what the hell she thought she was doing. This girl was more than likely underage—Malone would get around to asking—and she was most likely a runaway. And it was equally likely that she was running away from something very mean and dangerous. Malone would get around to asking that as well. For now, she had to keep the girl from running into worse danger than she'd left. The world was full of predators.

"I've got to get water to my mare. Your first job is to go in and make sure things are on and working … lights, water heater, refrigerator, which is probably empty, but we'll worry about that later." Malone pulled out the key chain she'd slipped into her pocket earlier and held it out to her stowaway.

With clear reluctance, the girl took it and started toward the house. Halfway there, she stopped to look back at Malone. "How much are you paying?"

Malone matched her look for look. "We'll negotiate

later. Get moving."

As she'd expected the girl responded immediately to that tone of authority. She wasn't a renegade or a rebel, then, just a little girl lost. Malone watched her walk away, Callahan at her heels, and realized she didn't even know her name.

* * *

I don't imagine there's much in the way of a decent meal anywhere near, but like myself, the young girl's first thoughts turn to food. First stop, the kitchen, painfully clean. No one has cooked here in a while. While she rummages through the cabinets, I make a tour of the other rooms. I sense no other human presence, but better to be safe than be taken by surprise. Besides, there's very little that can be found in a cupboard that will catch my interest. Boxes are blah and tins of food have to be opened and heated before they appeal to me. And they have to contain some kind of meat … that's a given.

Room by empty room. At least empty of recent human inhabitance. Furnishings, more than I expected, but clean and bare of any clutter. Someone took the time to clear away any mementos. No photographs in frames. No magazines or books lying about. But, even so, there's a story told in the polished wood furnishings and chenille bedspreads with filmy curtains over windows that overlook the hills beyond. Whoever passed their years here had an eye to need and comfort rather than any fashion of the moment. I could feel right at home here, at least in the short term.

On my return to the kitchen, I find the girl leaning against a counter, staring out a window unframed by curtains. I leap lightly to the counter, careful to land some distance away so as not to startle her. I peek through the window as well and together we watch as Malone walks purposefully toward the house.

Chapter 3

Cade accepted Kelli's offer of the last cup of coffee in the carafe and she returned to the kitchen for a refill. With Malone on her way to Georgia, he'd had no need to flee the premises and had joined Frank's impromptu breakfast party with several other lingering wedding guests. He wondered when he'd gotten to be such a coward, that a woman could make him bolt. But Malone wasn't just any woman. Malone was … Malone.

He wished again that he hadn't seen her up close and personal, hadn't felt the warmth of her skin beneath his hands when she'd turned and stepped into him. Her shoulders had been silky smooth, and it would be a long time before he forgot the light scent of the fragrance she'd been wearing. Hell, who was he kidding? He wouldn't forget. He would simply store the encounter along with all of his other memories of her.

Kelli returned to the dining room with the carafe in one hand, her cell phone in the other, and an odd look on her face. She looked at Frank who sat opposite of Cade. "That was Malone."

Kelli's expression and tone, as well as the mere mention of Malone's name put Cade on alert, but he stayed silent as she continued, "It seems that Callahan … Dax's gray cat … hitched a ride in her trailer. She found him when she got to her grandfather's property and wanted me to let Dax know he was fine, and she'd get him back when she could."

"But?" Frank asked studying her expression.

"Honestly? I don't know. She sounded … distressed … maybe, but when I asked if something was wrong, she said no, that she was tired." Faint lines of disquiet creased Kelli's forehead. "Honestly? I felt like she wasn't telling me everything and that the something she wasn't sharing was a concern."

Cade would have given a small fortune to hear the tone of Malone's response for himself. A glance around told him that Frank felt the same. The atmosphere in the room had turned from festive to concerned.

"Who is Dax? One of the wedding guests?"

"No but he would have been welcome to come. All of the hands were. Dax started out just as a handyman, but it didn't take long to figure out that he had a knack for leadership … maybe something he did in the service. The others just seem to look to him to give direction and keep them moving and productive so I made him foreman. He just laughed, but he seems to appreciate the raise."

"But the cat's nothing special, right?"

"He's cute. Has those funny folded ears. But, no." Kelli hesitated, then added, "Whatever is wrong isn't really to do with the cat."

"But you don't know anything is wrong," Frank said. "Not really."

Kelli shrugged. "My gut—and Malone's tone—tells me there is…"

That was all Cade needed. He stood decisively and looked at Frank. "You two have a plane to catch. Make sure you're on it. I'm going to see what's going on with Malone." It was what he wanted to do deep down at his core, and that made it easier for him to act on the improbable premise that a cat had stowed away with Malone because she was in danger of some kind.

Kelli gave an audible sigh of relief. "That would ease my mind, Cade, thank you so much."

Cade took his leave in short order. He didn't bother admitting to Kelli that his purpose in making the trip was far less for Kelli's peace of mind than for his own.

* * *

It's entertaining to watch these two females dance—conversationally speaking—around each other in Malone's quest for the truth. I'm listening hard because I'm still convinced there's some kind of trouble following the younger of the two. It's as clear to me as the heartache that follows the older woman. I hope I'll hear a hint of what hazards might lie ahead. The more information I have, the faster I can react.

* * *

Malone placed a glass of tea in front of her stowaway. So far, the girl had volunteered nothing except the fact that the refrigerator was running but bare of food as were the pantry and cabinets. Malone, who'd expected as much, had retrieved a few items from the tiny kitchen space in the living quarters of her trailer.

"Let's start with you telling me your name."

"Joss."

Malone didn't know whether to believe her or not. "Just Joss?"

"Yes."

"Last name," Malone prodded.

The girl hesitated. "Anything I tell you will be a lie."

Malone gave a short burst of laughter that faded quickly. "Well, that's honest. What or who are you afraid of?"

"What I was running from."

Ignoring her stubbornness, Malone propped her elbow on the table, chin in hand, studying the dark bruising along the girl's cheekbone. "Who hit you?"

"My husband."

"You aren't old enough to be married."

"My folks didn't think so either. That's why we ran off together."

That struck a strong chord in Malone though she hadn't gotten married and Tyge had never laid a hand on her in violence. But there was something too steady, too detached in the girl's words and Malone suspected they were no more than that. Just words. A story invented and memorized for exactly a moment such as this. She tested the waters. "So, you got married too young and he couldn't take the pressure and took it out on you with his fists."

Joss shrugged. "It happens."

"But not to you," Malone said softly.

It took only a heartbeat for the girl to realize that Malone was calling her on the made-up story, but as she tensed to rise, Malone placed a hand on hers. "I'm not going to do anything to put you in harm's way, but I'm not going to pretend I believe that tale of yours. Your first words to me were 'don't tell them where I am.' *Them* not *him*, not some made up husband."

The girl leaned back in her chair but didn't bother to argue the point. Malone could see the weariness and creeping despair in the rich hazel eyes.

"Whoever they are, I won't give you away. Just don't run, okay? You're safer here with me and Callahan than anywhere outside these walls. I promise."

At her words, Joss glanced at the cat. "He's hungry, I think."

Malone interpreted that to mean the girl was hungry … and that she didn't plan to bolt, at least not for the time being. Pushing aside the questions that clamored in her mind, she rose to her feet. "I turned the water heater on so we'll be able to shower soon. After we eat, I'll dig out some clothes that should come close to fitting you. You're as tall as I am, but they may be a bit loose on you."

"Why are you helping me?"

For a moment, Malone just looked at her then she sighed. "Because I can. Because you need it." It wasn't a complete answer, but it was all she could offer. If she tried to get Joss to some kind of official help, she hadn't a doubt in the world that the girl would run and land who-knew-where.

* * *

Huh! We learned exactly nothing in that back-and-forth except the fact that this Joss is not an accomplished liar which, from my point of view at least, is a good thing to know. Although panic can make the mildest of souls a hazard to themselves and others, I don't think—at this point—I need to keep an eye on her for anything except the risk of her doing a runner. She's not a danger to Malone. I am, however, confident that danger threatens her.

It would take a particularly nasty person to strike a young lady in the face. And though she matches Malone in height, young is the appropriate word. Young and vulnerable though she bears a quiet dignity that a few others, much older than her, would do well to mimic.

So now I have to figure out how to defend her from whatever unknown threat might come. From any direction. Piece of cake. While I await a much-needed lunch, I'll do another recon of the house, this time with an eye to protecting the two females that fate has pushed into my care.

The rooms in this house are an interesting design but not the most defensible. Most are unexpectedly connected so that—although there's a central hallway as well—it's almost possible to make a full circle of the house from room to room. Hmmm. A curtain is lifted ever so slightly by a breeze in the far bedroom. Although there's only the slimmest opening at the bottom, the window itself is low enough to the ground that an intruder could easily lift it and gain silent access. I'll have to bring this to Malone's attention. Fortunately, I don't sense anything sinister here. It's plain the house, though vacant, has had caretakers. Someone was careless, no doubt, but should some wrongdoer come looking for an easy way in, I'd rather they be obligated to break a glass or force a lock. Either of those would be equally noisy, giving warning of their presence.

* * *

When Callahan came to get her—and there wasn't any doubt in Malone's mind that that was exactly his intent—Malone followed much more promptly than she might have prior to this morning's worrisome phone call about Tyge combined with the unexpected arrival of Joss into her orderly though fast-paced existence.

As Callahan led her down the hall it occurred to her, that as satisfying as her career was to her and as exciting the world of rodeo might seem to others, she'd gotten very comfortable with being alone, responsible only for the horses—her own and those entrusted to her by others—and herself. It was work, hard work, but it was gratifying labor. Sure, there was heartache but also quiet pleasures and breathtaking successes.

Suddenly, unexpectedly, she'd had thrust upon her a girl patently too young to be on her own and a gray cat who seemed more human than some humans she knew. Malone wasn't foolish enough to discount the possibility. She'd lived close to horses for too many years not to realize there were depths to animals that some people never discerned.

When Callahan led her straight to the farthest bedroom and a window that someone had left open the tiniest bit, she closed and latched it securely, feeling a flare of anxiety that someone could be hiding in wait. She turned to the bed where the sleek feline sat watching her with a very steady yellow-gold gaze.

"Should I be alarmed? Is there anything else I need to check?" She felt foolish for asking, but still—

Callahan rose to stretch and circle slowly before he lay

down and closed his eyes.

Malone chuckled and said, "Guess not."

Callahan swished his tail just a bit then curled it around him. His eyes remained closed.

And I am dismissed, Malone thought.

* * *

Lunch wasn't terrible, but a trip into town will be a good thing as I have hopes we'll return with something more than not terrible. But, of course, Malone has to check and double-check that her horses continue safe and happy in their surroundings as appears to be the case. I wonder if she noticed that Joss appears more than a little comfortable in the presence of the very large animals. I deduce this was not our runaway's first close-up encounter with that species.

As I settle myself on the comfortable back seat of the truck, I debate if the time required for the drive will allow for a snooze. But, no, Malone advises Joss that they need only the local feed store and small grocer in a nearby community. Her horses must have fresh hay for a night or two and we, of course, must have a decent supply of provisions.

I feel vindicated that Malone acknowledged my superior abilities about the open window so quickly. Rarely do humans ask my advice within the first day of our acquaintance. She also seemed to understand my response that no, there was no cause for alarm nor anything she needed to check or do beyond securing that window. Even with that, I don't think for a minute that she recognizes the depth of my abilities. I have a number of tricks worth a whole lot more than checks for minor security breaches. Hopefully, there won't be any need for her to learn the true and far-reaching extent of my skills. But we'll see. Here I am and here I'll stay until convinced there's no danger to this extremely independent barrel racer.

I hear Malone comment to Joss upon the girl's apparent comfort with her horses and I settle into my nap, pleased at such an observant nature. My work is always much easier when the humans around me are aware and perceptive.

* * *

"Have you broken any laws?" Despite Joss's reticence, Malone was working on a need-to-know basis. Some questions had to be asked and answered. Non-negotiable.

"No, ma'am." The lack of hesitation and calm in Joss's response was reassuring.

"Where's your family?"

"I don't have any." Before Malone could challenge her on that, Joss added very softly, "Not anymore." And Malone left that heartache alone.

"Is anyone going to be looking for you?"

For a while Malone thought she wouldn't answer, but she finally admitted, "Maybe. I don't know. I don't think so, but, if they do, I'll kill or be killed, but I won't go with them."

Malone felt a chill down her spine. Them, again. Plural. That had an ugly sound to it. She sighed, not happy with the complicated turn her life had taken. Nothing to do about it now, because she couldn't put the girl out on the street.

Time to turn the subject. "You've spent time around horses?"

"Once upon a time. Not so much this past year."

"How well do you ride?"

"Better than most, not as well as some."

"Barrels?"

Joss shook her head. "Brush track racing. I jockeyed for trainers. But not on race day."

Malone heard the slightest edge of resentment in the last part. There remained a lot of discrimination against female athletes in every sport. Barriers were being broken but slowly.

"Well, here's what I can offer you for now. Food in your stomach, but you'll be expected to help cook and clean up after. A roof over your head, most often in the living quarters of my horse trailer as I'm on the road a lot. A little cash in your pocket." She named a by-the-day figure she could afford and seemed fair when coupled with room and board.

"In return for?"

Malone glanced over to find herself being watched with more than a trace of suspicion.

"Maybe exercising horses since you've got the skill, but I'll have to watch you first," she cautioned. "Grooming, cleaning stalls, all the things I have to do each and every day. I'm only in LaGrange for a day or two then I'm headed back to Oklahoma City for a last run before the circuit finals in Montgomery. I've got horses to pick up along the way—more than I usually try to take on in the same trip— but I've ridden them to success this year and I'm being paid well to run them in the finals. I can use the help although I'd planned to do without, so it's up to you."

"I feel safer here. Maybe I could just stay in that house until you get back. Take care of it and all. You wouldn't have to pay me anything. I could get a job in town, maybe."

"Well, my plan right now is to put that property on the market." But even as Malone said the words, she felt something deep inside tugging her in a different direction.

Regardless, she wasn't about to leave a young teen there alone. "You don't have a way to get to and from a job. Besides it wouldn't be long until someone figured out you were there and called the authorities."

Joss huffed and the sound of teen frustration brought a smile to Malone's lips though this certainly wasn't a matter for much levity.

Malone pulled into a parking place in front of the feed store and turned to look at Joss. "I'll keep you as safe as I can, as safe as I keep the horses in my care, but the more information I have about who or what might come looking for you, the better I can do at that."

Joss met her look steadily and said, "I don't know. I'll think about it."

Malone wasn't sure if Joss meant she'd think about the job or owning up to what she faced, but Malone held her peace. She had a strong-willed girl on her hands. She ought to know. It felt a bit like looking into a mirror from her own distant past. Except she'd been running *to*, not running *from*.

They made a quick trip into the feed store and Joss proved she was no stranger to ranch work. Without hesitation, she jumped lightly into the back of the truck to catch and land a couple bags of feed followed by bags of stall shavings and bales of hay. All were tossed to her by a young man who looked like he wanted to flirt. Though Joss kept as much of her hair stuffed under that well-worn ball cap as she could, Malone noted it did nothing to hide the fact that she was very much a girl and a pretty one at that. Regardless, the young man's efforts to catch her attention got no encouragement from Joss.

After gathering horse supplies, they shifted gears and

walked into a rather quaint market which had all they needed and then some.

Not until they were settled into the truck with their few bags of food did Malone check her phone and reluctantly listen to the single phone message. Tyge's voice, his tone of despair caught her like a throat punch. "Malone? Babe? Are you okay?" There was a long pause and for a moment she thought he'd broken the connection with just that. "I'm so damned sorry about this mess. Let me hear from you. Please, Malone."

The sound of weariness at the end affected her even more than the initial desperation. Good God in heaven, what had Tyge done this time? And what did it have to do with her?

With Joss's curious gaze fixed on her, Malone hit redial, but the call went straight to voice mail. She didn't leave a message. What could she say?

With a shrug at Joss as if the call were of no consequence, Malone turned the key in the ignition. But inside, she was trembling with all too familiar anxiety. And she had never, ever wanted to feel this way again. Vowed she never would.

Chapter 4

Malone pulled back into her grandparents' drive—would she ever consider this place anything but theirs?—saw and recognized Cade's truck pulled to one side and stifled whatever feeling stirred somewhere deep within her. She sensed Joss's quick tension and said, "Friend, not foe," before she stepped out of the truck and started pulling bags out of the back seat. The friend part wasn't quite accurate, but whatever Cade was to her, he was not her enemy.

Anything Joss might be thinking, feeling, she hid it well as she helped Malone with the bags. And, with her own nerves on edge from Joss's precipitous entrance into her life, Tyge's ominous phone message, and now Cade's unexpected appearance, all Malone wanted to do was get a grip so she didn't fall apart. Not here and not now. Not in front of Cade.

* * *

All things considered, the trip into town proved productive and enlightening, at least as far as the character of the woman I find in need of my talents. Nosing through the market bags during our return trip, I find not one package of dry cat food and not a single can filled with smelly ingredients. What a cat likes won't be found in a bag or can. That kind of protein might cover basic needs, but that's about it. I'm beginning to believe this Malone understands a cat's tastes and is savvy enough to ignore false advertising. Seriously, if a human wouldn't eat it, why do they think a cat would?

As we all step from the heights of this rather massive truck, I hear her tiny sound of dismay as she casts another glance at the truck. I recognize the shape and smell of it as belonging to Cade and agree with her that he isn't a foe. But neither am I alarmed by his presence as she seems to be. I am, however, curious that he's not waiting in the truck and feel confident he wouldn't be the type to enter her home uninvited even if he found the front door unlocked, which it was not. I turn from watching her open the aforementioned door and saunter in the direction of the barn and paddock.

Saunter. I like that word. I heard it on one of Dax's videos. It conveys my confidence in my assessment of the situation as well as my certainty that I can manage any troublesome circumstance that might arise. At the other end of the spectrum, I'm just as capable of lethal speed and use of force when and if I find either a necessity. And sometimes they are.

I spy Cade with both arms propped against a fence rail watching Malone's horses as they graze. I've gotten attuned to equine nuances during a few of Dax's odd jobs. Those tasks haven't all had to do with grass-eaters, whether cattle or horses, but there's been enough to acquaint me with their likes and dislikes. This large specimen is comfortable with human presence close by but uneasily attentive to the animal sitting quietly at his side. I can tell this by the twitching of the ears in that direction from time to time as if to gauge any threatening movement.

Those ears prick forward and, though the steed's head does not lift, the grazing ceases as the dog stands at my approach.

Without turning, Cade murmurs a quiet, "Whoa, Townsend."

And, what, I might ask is a handle like Townsend to give a canine? Gleaming—though oddly patterned—black and white fur and a fit physique aside, this is still a dog. And, generally speaking, I don't much care for dogs. They bark at inopportune moments and frequently have to be reminded of their place with a quick swipe of an extended claw—or two.

This one, I'm pleased to note, listens to the softly spoken command of his master, but my final judgement of his character is on hold until I know him better.

* * *

Cade waited for Malone to come to him. He'd heard her truck pull in, truck doors opening and closing. She wouldn't have missed the presence of his own pickup parked at one side of the drive.

He sensed the gray cat before he saw him, watched as the feline leapt to a fat, corner post. Large golden eyes stared back at him without blinking. The much-praised Callahan, no doubt. That gold stare shifted from his only when Townsend's tail began to whip in greeting as Malone walked up.

"Hi."

One husky word from her and years blinked out of existence. He saw them squared off as they'd been so long ago, experienced once again his frustration saw the mix of anger and hurt on her face. He couldn't count the times he'd regretted those moments, the heated, cutting words that had sent them spinning in opposite directions.

"I was wrong." It wasn't exactly what he'd intended to say, but once the words were spoken, he wasn't sorry.

"Yes." For a moment, he thought she would stop there, with that single acknowledgement of his fault, his failure. Then she added, softly, "And I wasn't old enough or wise enough to know what I didn't know." She broke their eye contact and turned to look out across the paddock. "But I suspect you didn't drive all this way to tell me that."

"No, but I should have. I'm proud of you, Malone. Of who you are and what you've made of yourself. Your success." He wasn't just talking about the fact that she'd managed to make a really good living in an industry that was as demanding, as competitive, and as heartbreaking as any athletic sport on national television. She'd done it with grace and style. And she'd done it alone, succeeding despite her ex-boyfriend.

"Thank you."

Her profile was to him, her attention fixed on the horse in the paddock. He couldn't tell if his words mattered to her at all. Wasn't sure how he felt about saying them but didn't regret that he had. It was past time they made peace with each other.

A brisk wind sent a scrap of paper toward the mare. She snorted and shied away from it in play, prancing halfway around the pen for good measure before settling again to graze on the last grass of summer.

Malone's lips curved in a faint smile that faded when she turned back to Cade. "So why *are* you here, Cade?"

He tilted his head toward the gray cat sitting motionless and watchful on the corner post. "To find out what that cat knows and make sure you're in no danger."

"As you can see, I'm fine. You can head back out with a clear conscience."

He ignored the suggestion. "How long are you staying in LaGrange?"

Her glare held pure exasperation. "I don't need taking care of, Cade. I never did." It was a deliberate jab.

Cade wanted to tangle with her over his motives on that long-ago and very ill-fated day, but now wasn't the time or place. "I promised Frank and Kelli I'd check things out here. If I hadn't, they would be standing here themselves instead of relaxing in a first-class cabin on a jet headed to Wales." It wasn't his only motive by a long shot. Still, it was a true statement and succeeded in taking the starch out of her shoulders. He didn't see much need to go any deeper into his reasons, not now. Maybe not ever.

He waited—patiently for him—until she turned her attention from the red mare he suspected she wasn't really seeing at this point, to him. "So, why don't you tell me why the cat decided you needed his company?"

Malone hesitated for a long, long moment before admitting, "I had a stowaway in my horse trailer. Callahan must have been prowling around the hatches and saw something because he somehow ended up coming along for the ride as well."

The skin tightened on the back of Cade's neck. Only the fact that Malone was beside him, unscathed by any encounter, kept Cade from a sharp rejoinder. At least verbally. Internally, was a different matter. The hell she didn't need taking care of.

He watched as the gray cat had nonchalantly lifted one paw to begin grooming himself. "And just where is that *stowaway* now?"

"She's inside. At least I hope she is. She's a flight risk and I won't put it past her to slip out a back window and run if she thinks you're a threat. She barely trusts me."

She. Some of Cade's tension eased, but only some. "Is she running from the law?"

"I don't think so. She's got a few bruises, blamed them on an ex-husband, but she's lying about that."

"Husband? How old is she?"

"If she's sixteen, I'll be surprised."

"So, she's run away from home."

"I'm not sure about that part. She's hiding, but I don't have a clue from who or what. I'm planning on looking up some recent Amber Alerts to see if I can find anyone who looks or sounds like her. She got on board in Lake Charles, but I don't know if that's where she's from."

"Have you called the authorities?" Somehow, knowing Malone, he'd already surmised the answer to that.

"No, and I'm not going to."

"You could be putting yourself into some real legal difficulties here, Malone."

"And I could do worse than that if I do call them. They'll contact some state department who'll come after that girl. They'd never get her into a vehicle with them, not without force, which means I'd be arrested for fighting them off her."

Cade rubbed the back of his neck, battling every wrong word he wanted to say.

Unexpectedly, Malone smiled though her gaze retained just a bit of poignancy. "You always did that when you were getting ready to lecture me."

"I'm not going to lecture you, Malone."

"What *are* you going to do?"

"Damned if I know." And damned if he did. "Maybe a better question is, what are you going to do?"

He wasn't surprised when Malone pushed away from the fence rail and said, "Right now I'm going to unload feed and make sure my horses have a safe, comfortable place for the next two nights."

* * *

Malone tried not to think about spiders as she checked out a stall close to the barn door, but then again, thinking about spiders was almost preferable to thinking about Cade. She'd made herself *not* think about him for so many years that his presence was unnerving and every single memory, every moment of teen angst came flooding back. And it did no good to tell herself she was a different person now. She was not that seventeen-year-old half in love with, but furiously battling, a guy who had not the slightest idea what she needed or wanted from him. And she'd driven him away with bitter, angry words.

Somehow, somewhere inside of her, that younger self had expected Cade to realize his mistake and come after her, wrest her away from Tyge because he'd know, surely, he'd know, Malone didn't really love Tyge, didn't really plan to tie her life to his. She'd just desperately wanted out of a small-town future, out of her parent's plans for college, and into the world of rodeo. She'd packed her bags in the dead of that summer night and loaded her barrel horse beside Tyge's in his old two-horse trailer, with stars glittering in a midnight sky. Even as she reminded herself that Tyge believed in her, believed she could make it on the circuit, a part of her heart had hoped and watched and waited, looking back at the empty highway miles for those familiar headlights to come racing after her. But Cade, who'd strode away in fury, appeared to have taken her words to heart and he never came and life went on.

Halfway through Tennessee, in a roadside motel, she gave her virginity to Tyge, but she never quite gave him her heart.

And, now, when she didn't want him, didn't need him, Cade had reappeared, hefting feed bags and hay bales with ease, seeming not to notice the dust they left on crisp jeans and navy-blue polo with their association logo on the front. She tried not to notice *him*. After all these years, he was just someone she used to know.

But when their hands brushed as they both reached for the same water bucket, she pulled hers back as if she'd touched fire. And Malone had quit playing with fire years ago. Somehow, she had to get Cade on the road, on his way back out of her life. She had enough on her hands with whatever problem her stowaway had brought and whatever trouble Tyge had stirred up and seemed to fear might spill over onto her. At least Tyge had enough decency left to care about the possibility.

Cade had fallen silent as they worked together after asking only if she didn't want to put the feed and the hay in the barn. He'd nodded understanding at her quiet statement that she didn't plan to stay for long and was used to working between her trailer and whatever barn her horses were in. He, of course, understood living on the road.

For years Cade and his cousin had been top earners in team roping in their circuit, but he'd gradually transitioned from competition to management of a rival association. Recently, when he'd stepped up to become a director for the association where she still competed and paid her dues, she'd realized she would no doubt encounter him at some point. But she'd expected to be better prepared for the moment.

Malone found herself casting frequent glances toward the house, wondering each time if Joss was sliding out some back window, knowing there was nothing she could do about it if she were. The girl would stay and allow Malone to help her or she would go. Malone wouldn't take her choices from her, but she couldn't help the nagging worry and knew she'd carry it with her down the road if the girl left.

As they finished, Malone cast a look around the barn. The aged wood was solid, undoubtedly far stronger than what passed for lumber in more modern barns. The horses each had a large, safe stall for the next day.

She turned to look at Cade. "I appreciate the help."

"But you didn't need it."

"No, I didn't. And, as you can see, I'm fine and safely settled in now."

"Malone, I'm not leaving."

* * *

Hmmm, such tension in the air. I'll admit to being surprised when Malone doesn't bother to argue but simply turns on her heel and strides toward the house, leaving Cade to follow if he will. And, of course, he does with the devoted Townsend at his heels. Oh, and I can't keep to calling that dog by such a silly name, not with his tongue lolling happily out of his mouth as he prances at his master's side. Townsend, it can't be. Townie, perhaps? As in one of those poor suburbanites who have no inkling about serious outdoor living? Hmmm. That's a maybe. I'll try that for a bit to see if it fits, although, I'm not sure how long the duo will be staying. We'll just have to see who has the stronger motivation, Malone to send him on his way or Cade to remain in the event recent happenings are not as innocent as they seem.

I'm amazed even more to find Joss standing in the kitchen with her back to the counter. I rather thought she'd be hiding in a back room, waiting for the visitor to leave and hoping he'd go away without coming inside. Regardless of her youth, she has courage; I suspected she must by virtue of having fought and run rather than choosing to submit to whatever fate had been planned for her. Too often humans fear the unknown much more than the known, regardless of however unpleasant, even treacherous their circumstances may be. Felines never choose to remain in unwelcoming environments.

Malone performs the briefest of introductions, saying, "Joss, this is Cade."

And although Cade extends his hand, Joss's arms remain crossed in front of her. She watches him carefully, rather similar to the manner in which I might regard a snake that has slithered too close, not certain it's a threat, but neither certain it isn't, until it has passed me by without incident.

To his credit, Cade ignores the slight as he accepts a glass of tea from Malone and her offer of a seat at the well-used kitchen table.

To keep the overly friendly Townie from flouncing down on top of me, I leap to a corner of the counter beside Joss, who chooses not to join them at the table. I think she takes a bit of comfort from my presence though her shoulders stiffen as Cade fixes his gaze on her. "I'm not here to hurt you or allow you to be hurt, but I do need to know who will come after you," *he says. Oops, Malone is looking daggers at him.* "We need to know." *Heh, heh, fast—and wise—reaction to that very pointed look cast his way.*

* * *

Malone waited, smug in her certainty that Cade would have no better luck getting information from Joss than she had.

With the unerring accuracy of every teen ever, Joss deflected his next question by looking straight at Malone and asking, "Instead of focusing on me, why don't you tell him about the phone message? The one that made your hands shake."

Chapter 5

Cade held his temper, by a thread, but he managed. He might *not* have managed if he'd known where to unleash it. A part of him acknowledged that whatever was happening with Malone—whatever troubled her— was hers to resolve. Another part of him said, "hell no" to that. Maybe it was because of their past, their shared memories of good times and bad. Maybe it was because of feelings that had resurfaced at seeing her again, after years of keeping those feelings tightly contained. Maybe it was because he *was* the 'tyrannical despot' she'd once called him. Even at seventeen, Malone, who'd divided her time between horses and books, had owned an extensive and imaginative vocabulary.

Regardless, Cade wasn't just going to drive back the

way he'd come and leave Malone to whatever fate someone wanted to dish out to her. Nor did he trust one gray cat to protect her, despite Malone's suspicion that the cat was smarter than most, despite even the fact that Cade himself had been unpredictably and intrinsically reassured by Callahan's calm response to Malone's pronouncement that she'd found a stowaway on board her trailer.

To that end, he was patient through a meal a reluctant Malone invited him to share because she was too polite to ask him point-blank to leave. Patient as they talked about which ropers and rough stock riders and barrel racers were moving into which circuit finals, who might move on to the national finals the first week of January, what contestants had been successful the previous year but less so this year and the whys and wherefores. Idle chit-chat he could accomplish while his mind wrestled with how to keep Malone from harm when she didn't want his help. And the truth of the matter was that he couldn't. Couldn't when he was twenty-two, couldn't through the years since, couldn't now. Not unless she allowed him to and he didn't think that likely.

He noted Joss listened to their conversation but didn't offer a single word, answering only if asked a direct question. He'd never seen a person that young that quiet. But he'd also never seen a young girl with bruises across her face that may well have been from someone's fist. It clenched the muscles in his gut every time he glanced her way. Deep down he knew he'd sometimes feared that was Malone's fate after she'd run off with LaMonte. Cade had kept tabs, though and—despite Tyge's reputed propensity for using his fists instead of his wits in any dispute—Cade had never heard one word that he'd used them on Malone. LaMonte wouldn't be in one piece today if he had.

Dusk had lit the skies with purple and put the hills in shadows by the time he stepped out of the house, watching from the porch as Malone headed back out to feed the horses. She hesitated halfway along the path to the barn and glanced back as if she'd sensed his stare. She wore one of her grandpa's plaid flannel shirt-jackets and her hair spilled to her shoulders in a silken sheen of rich caramel. She'd never looked more vulnerable—or more beautiful—than she did in that moment.

Knowing it was a mistake before he ever made a move, Cade stepped off the porch to follow.

Watching Malone measure feed and supplements for her mare, the years fell away and Cade automatically reached for the pail when she closed the top of the feed bag. With a fathomless glance, she yielded it to him and separated a section of hay to take with her. They fell in step together as they walked the short distance from her trailer to the barn.

Jaz greeted them with a nicker, butting Cade's arm as he emptied the pail into her larger feed bucket. Malone talked softly to each horse as she fed, refilled water buckets, and used a forked scoop to clean stalls. She had yet to speak a word to Cade and—for the moment—he didn't mind the fact. If they weren't talking, they weren't arguing.

Malone latched the last stall door behind her and turned to face Cade. Her eyes searched his face as if looking for a hint as to his thoughts. "What now?" she asked at last.

Cade didn't bother with words. He leaned in and brushed her mouth with his, not daring to pull her in close and hard against him, though he longed to do just that. For too brief a moment, he felt her lips soften and yield before she stepped back and away.

"No." That one soft word was all she said then she turned and walked back to the house.

No was right. Cade knew it, even agreed with it on some level. But there were other, more visceral levels where he did not. There was a lifetime of experiences between who they were now and who they had been. Instead of giving way to the temptation to touch her, taste her, he should've taken the moment to ask whose phone call had the ability to make her hands shake. She wasn't likely to give him that opportunity now, much less give him an answer.

Townsend bumped his leg and he looked down at the ball the dog carried in his mouth and Cade spent the next half hour burning his pent-up frustration and making his dog ecstatic.

The house was dark and quiet when he went back inside with Callahan and Townsend. He bolted the door and found a spare bedroom by the simple act of walking past two doors which were solidly closed and into the first one that stood open. There'd be hell to pay if his folks knew he'd come back this way after the wedding and not come by, but he'd spent several pleasant days with them beforehand and there just wasn't time for it now.

* * *

Although she'd planned to stay at least one more day, Malone had the trailer loaded and what now seemed like an entourage on the road well before noon. She gave a last glance around the old farmstead and knew she wasn't ready to make a decision on what to do with the place. It was home to her in a way no other place had ever been. She had enough regrets in her past, she wouldn't add to that by acting in haste—not when she could help it. There was time for her to be sure of her own mind. She would give herself that time.

Cade didn't press her for any more information, didn't give her any advice, but she knew in her heart she hadn't seen the last of him and not just because they belonged to the same association now. Whatever they were or weren't, they had a past. Although she didn't intend for them to have a future, they had a past.

To her relief, Cade didn't try to hang with her as she headed back west. When she made her first exit to stop for fuel, she saw his truck hold steady on the interstate. She took a deep breath and squared her shoulders. Time for her to focus on the competition ahead, on giving one hundred percent to each horse and each run.

As they traveled, with Joss riding shotgun and Callahan stretched out on the back seat, Malone gave Joss control of the radio, found they liked the same station, same songs. The girl had a soft contralto voice, unusual enough in itself, but also one that was far above average. "You could be the next Reba McEntire or Jennifer Nettles." Malone was only half kidding.

Joss flashed her a half-smile. "I'd aim for Miley Cyrus. Or maybe Bonnie Tyler."

"So, you understand your voice and music." That seemed odd to Malone. Most teens were more into the lyrics than an understanding of vocal range and which singers were what.

Joss's smile disappeared. "My mom taught me. She named me after Joss Stone. She called her Britain's version of a soul singer."

"I'm familiar with her." But Malone was more

interested in Joss's mention of her mother and the sadness that accompanied her comments.

"Where is your mother now, Joss?"

"St. Luke's Cemetery."

Malone felt the weight of Joss's sadness but also the absence of any faith. Not heaven. Not hell. St. Luke's Cemetery.

"I'm sorry for that. You miss her."

"I miss a lot of things. But life goes on and I will too."

Malone could agree with that and she didn't press further, didn't have the inclination, and didn't really have time when her phone rang. She glanced at the truck display, saw Tyge's name and photo flash, and hesitated. She wasn't sure what was up with him. With Joss's presence in mind, she hit accept, hoping he'd at least mind his language. "You're on speaker, Tyge. I'm on the road with a friend."

"Are you okay?" He sounded edgy.

"I'm fine." She kept her tone relaxed despite a rush of anxiety. "What's going on with you? I got your voice mail and tried to call you back."

"Yeah, I turned it off for a while when I couldn't get you. I just need to know you're okay."

"I'm fine. Who are you hiding from?" *And what have you done now?*

"Don't tell them where I am. Don't tell them anything."

"Tyge, I don't *know* where you are. And who is *them?*"

"Just be careful, okay, babe?"

Malone sighed as Tyge cut the connection. He hadn't answered her questions and she hadn't expected him to.

She felt Joss staring at her and wasn't surprised when the girl said, "Seems like I'm not the only one with a problem."

"No," Malone agreed softly, "seems like you're not."

She thought of her empty search through recent, and some not so recent, Amber Alerts. Her laptop, brought in from the living quarters of the trailer, had yielded nothing. No one was looking for a girl matching Joss's description, at least not openly. Malone took comfort from the thought that no one who wished Joss harm could possibly know where she was now or who she was with. They had traveled miles and cities and states away from where she had first slipped aboard Malone's trailer and they were headed even further away.

An unexpected thought caused a frisson of alarm. "Do you have a cell phone?"

"Had one. Threw it away so they couldn't use it to find me."

"Smart girl."

"No way to pay for the service at the end of the month anyway."

Malone glanced at her and then away, dismayed. Malone had run away from home, it was true, but she'd never had to run away from danger.

* * *

Hmmm, what kind of man is Tyge? For that matter, what kind of name is that? Short for Tiger? An animal known to be graceful but deadly? Humph, doubtful. From his comments, I'd say this Tyge is more fearful for himself than for Malone. But he did, at least, ask about her well-being. If he's a forerunner for danger, I'll have to be doubly watchful. To that end, I commit the image of the man that appeared in the corner of the phone screen. Useful gadgets, these cell phones.

Chapter 6

Cade parked behind the show office, a long building with plenty of windows, and stepped out. He waited while Townsend leapt down behind him before closing and locking the door of the cab of his truck. Though it was days early for most of the contestants to arrive, there were several trucks and trailers scattered around the parking areas marked for big rigs. He studied the acres of asphalt and security lighting that fronted both the office building and the coliseum. Beyond were barns and paddock areas.

Cade felt more anxious than he'd anticipated he might in this moment. He'd moved the venue for the Southeast Circuit Finals, initially amid protests from every other member of the board. It was a business decision and he'd convinced most of them he was right, especially when he'd shown them the math. Plain and simple, Montgomery, Alabama had more to offer in terms of convenience for the competitors as well as for their followers. The newly built coliseum could house twice the number of fans. Last year they'd lost significant revenue because they'd been forced to turn away potential ticket-buyers which meant fewer customers for the vendors who were, in large part, their sponsors.

The city, and surrounding area, had things to offer as well. While there was little in the way of real tourist attractions, there were decent hotels and plenty of restaurants, even one or two that could boast fine dining. Despite his own good intentions, he pictured himself escorting Malone, dressed as she'd been the evening of the Hannas' wedding, into one of the nicer establishments. He had a quick unexpected vision of her as he'd last seen her, in jeans and boots, loading her mare onto the trailer and he smiled. He'd take Malone Summers anywhere in any attire.

For a moment, he wondered if thoughts of Malone had conjured an image of the gray cat sitting at the door of the show office. But no, at his approach, the image stood and stretched and cast him a look that would have been withering under any circumstances. Cade felt a touch of humor as he realized the crushing look was directed at Townsend. His greater reaction, however, was sheer pleasure at the knowledge that Malone was somewhere close.

She was not, he soon discovered, in the show office. His searching glance confirmed that. He turned that glance on the cat, wondering, but only for a moment. Callahan could not possibly have known to watch for him here. The cat must have accompanied Malone when she checked in that morning and somehow lost track of her. Unlike Townsend, cats were independent cusses. That was probably the real reason he'd ended up in Malone's rig to begin with. Cade would send Malone a quick text to let her know Callahan's whereabouts as soon as he checked in with the staff.

Big grins greeted Cade as he stepped behind the long counter. His assistant, a tall redhead with unmatched efficiency, waved a sheet of paper. "We're a sellout, boss." Her grin broadened. "You did it."

Cade smiled in return, allowing himself to enjoy the moment with her. Tried and true rodeo fans had followed them to the new venue and they'd added new enthusiasts, doubling the potential profits for their sponsors. That would lead to increased sponsorships down the road. After a brief exchange with the team, who had a whirlwind few days in front of them as contestants arrived and checked in, he asked which office was his and was gestured toward a corner door. He headed that way, Townsend and Callahan close at his heels.

A stack of reports waited for him in the sizeable room Aleta had selected to serve as his office for the duration of the event. He took a moment to send Malone a text concerning Callahan's current location before he settled into business. He hadn't gotten very far into the first report when his assistant tapped at his door, a curious expression on her face. "You've got a visitor, Mr. Delaney. May I show him in?"

A look of affront crossed her face as the *visitor* stepped past her and into the room without waiting for an invitation.

Despite the plain clothes, Cade recognized the crisp air of authority in every aspect of the man and said, "Thank you, Aleta. If you'd close the door…?"

The young woman gave him a searching look then nodded as if satisfied by his lack of alarm.

Cade gestured towards one of the chairs pushed into a corner. "How can I help you, Officer…?"

"Deputy U.S. Marshal James Ryder." The man said the words simply, not officiously before he handed Cade his badge, not questioning how Cade recognized him as law enforcement.

After a cursory look, Cade handed it back. He gave the deputy marshal a longer look. He judged him to be in his late thirties to early forties with a decade or two of experience in piercing brown eyes.

Ryder pulled one of the chairs closer to Cade's desk and sat down. He leaned back with a casual air clearly intended to be disarming.

"I understand you're the director here."

"I'm one of the directors of this association," Cade agreed, "Director of Operations." That title and the roles and responsibilities it carried put him in a lead position, it was true, but Cade didn't see a need to comment on the fact.

"So definitely a person who'd want to know about possible criminal activity within your rank and file."

Cade glanced toward the gray cat who now sat erect on the padded seat of the second chair. The tip of his tail, curled around him, twitched once as he returned Cade's look. Not possible, Cade thought to himself. The cat's movement and eye contact were coincidental and not a reaction to the comment. "I take it you don't mean the routine barroom brawl with busted tables and broken glass and maybe a broken bone or two."

"I don't, no."

"Names?"

Ryder hesitated. "Names can't be a part of this discussion. It's too early in the investigation with more unanswered than answered questions. That's what I'm looking for now. Answers." Cade had a feeling the marshal didn't give names because he didn't have them. He was fishing. "I'd like access to any information you have on your contestants and your vendors."

Cade leaned back in his chair and stifled a sigh. "I can't allow that."

"Even though you know I can get them…" Ryder let the sentence trail off suggestively.

"… through proper channels and proper methods," Cade finished for him.

Ryder did nothing to suppress his own exhalation of annoyance. "We're not talking penny ante stuff here, Delaney."

"Well then, ask me something I can answer or give me something I *can* do."

The deputy marshal got to his feet and handed Cade a business card. "Call me if you see anything you don't like."

Cade almost laughed—would have if he weren't feeling so grim inside—at the thought of all the things he'd witnessed over the years that he hadn't liked. "Give me a clue where to focus, at least."

Ryder gave him a hard look. "Trailers intended for horses and cattle can carry a hell of a lot more than livestock."

"Drugs?"

"And more."

"So why would a U.S. Marshal be involved in something typically handled by the DEA?"

"It's tied to another investigation." Ryder didn't wait for a response. Just nodded, turned, and walked out the door.

Cade sat for a moment, wondering what in blazes had just been dumped in his lap with the worst possible timing. This event—these contestants—commanded and deserved every bit of his concentration and effort. Now this. Damn.

* * *

Here we go, then. The hunt for the bad guy is on. Cade thinks he has clue number one handed to him by a very curt U.S. Marshal while my suspicion is that status belongs to the mysterious phone call from Tyge 'whoever' that left Malone so unnerved. It's up to me to make sure she confides whatever alarms her to Cade so that these two can begin to piece their knowledge together. Which, of course, is why I'm shadowing Cade. The more I know about his habits, the easier my work. I also think it's going to be up to me to determine if somehow Joss doesn't figure into this as the true clue numero uno. That's Italian for the number one for anyone less street smart than I've come to be after time on the road with Dax.

I can see the irritation building in Cade as he taps the lawman's business card against his desk. He gives me another of those steely, questioning glances as if he wished he could read my mind. No more than I, dude, no more than I. Most especially when dealing with non-felines. Too bad mindreading isn't an ability in the humans I help. However, there are other means of communication and I'm canny enough to find them when I need them.

Townie senses the tension in Cade as well. He watches his master and his tail swirls slightly.

Cade stands and reaches for his hat, a fine piece of western attire in grey, the same cool shade as his eyes. And out the door we go. Time for some action at last. Oomph! I hiss at the Aussie who is crowding me through the exit, his hair actually brushing against mine! It's clean hair, I'll give him that, but even so! I pause to give him my most fierce glare. I won't pretend to be surprised when it goes unheeded, as the clumsy dog bounces onto the sidewalk. Dogs have no finesse. This one brushes against me yet again and I growl very, very softly. He hesitates a heartbeat at the warning then wags his tail with unwarranted enthusiasm. Good Lord. Townie. Yeah, good name for him, as it turns out.

* * *

Cade strolled around the grounds with no particular destination in mind. The deputy marshal had given him far too much to think about and sitting in an office would have been no way to clear his mind. Although the traffic was still light, in a day or two every available inch would be taken, vehicles would get blocked, problems would need solving, and tempers would need soothing. Fortunately, that coordination wasn't his job. His was to ensure there were sufficient, and competent, staff whose job it was. He greeted the early arrivals by name but didn't linger with any of them until he bumped into one of the stock contractors who'd been with the association at its inception, as had Cade, each in a different capacity at the time, but the loyalty was there for both of them.

Nick Andrews had been one of the top steer wrestlers for a decade, taking the title three years running. A car wreck had derailed his career and he'd taken over his father's ranch, turning the focus from beef cattle to stock contracting for the sport he loved more than anything, even the wife who'd given it her best shot before leaving for a man who had never been on a horse.

Cade and Nick weren't bosom buddies but had that longstanding kind of friendship that allowed them to meet up after months, share a beer and a steak, and swap stories. They could comfortably enjoy each other's company for an hour or two and part ways until next time.

They exchanged greetings while Nick propped against the fender of his stock trailer and watched his oldest son ramrod the unloading of prime bulls with glossy coats and bright eyes. Unlike Nick, who was rarely without a sports coat and button-down shirt paired with impeccable jeans, the younger Andrews wore a long-sleeved tee shirt with the name of a rock band blazoned across the back. His jeans were strategically faded with frayed hems over sharp-looking boots.

"Marcus has turned into quite a hand," Cade commented. "How's your father doing? Did he come with you?"

"No, not this year. He's ornery as ever." Nick sighed and added, "but failing a bit, though I don't like owning up to that. He doesn't either for that matter. He's enjoyed his retirement so much, sits a horse as well and as often as ever, and keeps a keen eye on my boys as they work, still teaching them all he knows about cattle and loves doing it. But he's lost weight lately and that worries me, though doc says he's stronger than most his age. Still, this is the first time he's not made this trip with me. Just ain't like him, you know?"

They chatted a bit more about Nick's dad and Cade's parents before Cade circled the conversation closer to where he wanted it to go. "What do you think about the new group, Carlisle Contracting? Had much interaction with them?"

"Hauls the broncs only?" At Cade's nod, he said, "They seem okay. Quiet bunch. Mostly gals, did you notice? Found that odd but guess that's my age talking. Girls are taking over the world these days."

Cade laughed. "Probably do a better job of it than some of us have, but, yeah, that's the group. We signed them on less than a year ago. I've been trying to keep tabs on them. Haven't heard any gripes from the contestants but don't want to assume all is well just because no one wants to be first to complain."

Judging from Nick's expression, Cade knew he hadn't heard any grievances either, at least no more than the run of the mill gripes from those whose rides hadn't turned out well.

Nick confirmed that with a shrug. "Seem to be doing a good job providing solid, healthy stock that like their jobs. Don't think you can ask more than that. At least not if their paperwork is clean."

His tone and his glance turned questioning at the last comment and Cade was quick to reassure him. "Nothing of concern there. Business is legit and so are their dealings. They want a shot at the finals next year," he added by way of explanation. "They're on my 'wait and see' list, but I haven't ruled them out." But they were the newest of the contractors and Cade knew the least about them on a personal level. Of course, Ryder had mentioned contestants as well as vendors, but the association had hundreds of members. It wouldn't be possible to dig into each one of them. All Cade could do was question where he could and keep his eyes open, as the lawman had suggested.

Before Cade moved on, he said, "I heard the BlackJack has a mean porterhouse these days. Thought I'd check them out tonight."

Nick smiled broadly. "Hot damn. About seven?"

"Sounds good. See you there." Cade turned to leave but stopped when Nick spoke again.

"Uh, Cade?"

"Yeah?"

"Townsend's looking good, but when in blazes did you get a cat?"

Cade turned to glance at Callahan who was looking decidedly bored. "He belongs to a friend."

"Well, huh." Nick rubbed his jaw thoughtfully. "Didn't picture you for a cat-sitter. See you at the BlackJack."

* * *

Cat sitter is a low blow. The dog receives a compliment and I'm slapped with an insult. I guess that just shows the low level of intelligence to be found in some humans. I'm not sorry when Cade realizes it's time to resume our excursion.

I find most things of some interest, but cattle only in a limited capacity and only for a brief period of time. They don't have the athletic ability of horses. But they do have their uses, prime rib and top sirloin being my favorite two.

In my opinion it's past time we checked back in with Malone. That whole business has me feeling antsy. With a nudge and a bump at Cade's leg, I take the lead. Fortunately, he's able to understand simple commands and follows obediently in my wake. No doubt about it, he's getting wise to my elevated level of intelligence.

Once he spots Malone's rig ... and I think that's a peculiar name for a truck and trailer ... his step quickens and I lose my lead status. However, I'm not the least concerned by the fact. My superiority is clear in so many ways that I don't need evidence to prove it. Townsend remains simply—and I do mean simply—happy just to be in the presence of his master. That's the difference between dogs and cats. I don't have a master. I have a companion named Dax. We each have our unique set of survival skills so it's a decent partnership.

It doesn't take us long to reach Malone. Always efficient, I see she hasn't been idle in my absence though I don't think she's ever really idle. I watch as she effortlessly lifts a saddle from the back of a sleek looking animal. He's one of six that she has with her to ride here, although only one is here for the competition. The others are here because they travel with Malone everywhere she goes. It's a testament to Malone that her clients trust her with the best of their best.

Malone glances our way and gives a civil hello to Cade. Civil and patently cool, though not as chill as the front that blows from the north. I find myself grateful for my healthy covering of fur although I'm aware that tomorrow could dawn sunny and mild. That's one of the vagaries of these Southern states. With no urge to settle on cold ground, I leap to a folding chair that I doubt Malone has spared more than a minute to relax in.

Our Joss rounds the rear of the horse trailer and I can tell Cade doesn't immediately recognize the girl with her newly, and very inexpertly, shorn hair. Only a few wisps float out from under a warm cap the same nondescript olive green of her oversized jacket. Malone commented it was too large when they made the purchase, but Joss insisted, citing the extra length as her reason. If you ask me, it was the shapelessness that appealed to her. Just part of a clever disguise.

Just as recognition dawns on Cade, an insistent buzzing disturbs my comfort and I realize I share space with Malone's cell phone. The surface lights and I see the image of Tyge in the corner of her screen. This is my chance and it has to be brief! In the moment that I have, I expertly bat the phone into the air, hissing to catch Cade's attention.

Good man! He catches it mid-air and glances at the name. I see a hard gleam of recognition. Yep, I'm right, that's a name he knows and a person he holds in distaste. I've given him the hint and the opening. All I can do is hope he doesn't botch the deal at this point.

* * *

"Well done," Cade murmured to Callahan. He placed the phone in Malone's outstretched hand. "The phone call that made your hands shake? That was Tyge?"

"Both times," Joss offered, closing the distance between them.

Malone slipped the phone into her jacket pocket, giving first the cat, then the girl a reproving look, before glaring at Cade.

Joss ignored the look. "The second call was worse. When they actually talked."

"Joss." There was no mistaking Malone's tone of voice. It was clearly a warning.

The teen stared at her, blatantly unrepentant. "You're not afraid of anything. Nothing rattles you. I've been with you less than a week and watched you change a tire on the side of the interstate and stare down two dudes at a gas pump who tried to mess with you. But whatever is going on with this guy," she tilted her chin toward the pocket where the cell phone had disappeared, "has you uneasy. Not afraid, maybe, but jumpy for sure."

Cade battled with his temper, fought hard, before he allowed himself to cut in. "What's going on, Malone?"

"Nothing I can't handle. I've been handling things for a long time, Cade, all without help."

She said the words quietly and evenly. He wasn't sure if

it was meant as a dig, but he felt the bite of it all the same. He was wise enough not to argue, but he'd be damned if he wasn't going to hunt Tyge down and make him understand a few hard truths. And the thought of Malone facing down two strange guys bent on mischief chilled him to the bone. He couldn't discount the fact that, yeah, she'd been on her own a long time. Couldn't discount the fact that he'd been forced to put her out of his mind for a long time, that or go crazy. But he'd never been entirely successful there. He'd tucked her away as a memory and a regret. But she was back in the *here and now*, back with a vengeance.

He wasn't sure what he was going to do about the fact, but he damned sure wasn't going to ignore it.

Chapter 7

The BlackJack wasn't fine cuisine, but neither was it a hole-in-the-wall. The small, non-chain restaurant boasted a top-of-the-line chef who also happened to be the owner. Beer and wine were on the menu, but the offerings were also top of the line. If you wanted to drown your sorrows without emptying your wallet, this wasn't the place to come. Which was why Cade was surprised to see Tyge stroll in when he was half way through the perfectly seared steak on his plate.

They hadn't crossed paths in several years and Cade noted the changes from a dissolute lifestyle. A slight paunch above the belt buckle had replaced the hard, lean muscle of a pay-window cowboy. His face sagged more than his age warranted. Tyge bypassed the scattering of tables with their neat tablecloths and napkins folded around dinnerware, in favor of the bar. His gaze passed over the corner where Cade sat facing Nick without any sign of recognition.

Cade watched from the corner of his eye as Tyge took an empty barstool next to a small group of cowboys. He recognized some of them. Brax Roberts was a competitor, the older half of a father-son rope team. Somehow Cade wasn't surprised when Brax got to his feet shortly after Tyge took the seat next to him. He doubted the two had much in common to talk about. Tyge was a has-been. Brax had kept his competitive edge through some twenty years by working hard and living clean. Tyge said something Cade couldn't hear, but Brax shook his head and walked toward the door.

With fists itching to take a shot at his mug, Cade wished, honestly wished, for a few minutes in which he could be just another rodeo contestant instead of a director. A brawl of any sort was not something he could afford though it was something he damn sure wanted.

Looking up from his plate, Nick asked, "Something wrong with your steak?"

Cade picked up his fork. "No, for a second I thought I saw someone I knew. The steak here is as excellent as I remember. Glad the owner added porterhouse to the menu."

"Yeah, it's gotten hard to find most places."

They finished their meal in companionable conversation and parted at the front door of the establishment. Nick was parked out front, Cade in the back. The night was starkly cold though the earlier wind had dropped, making the temperature less unbearable. Beyond the glow of the street lights, the dark seemed absolute, testimony that the thick layer of clouds still hugged close to the earth.

While Nick pulled away from the curb, Cade made a slow circle around the restaurant and walked right back in the front door to the small bar where two or three lone patrons ate first class steak and drank first rate beer. The bronze pendants over the bar cast a warm glow across the inhabitants. Tyge didn't look half as disreputable in the hazy light.

Cade slid onto the one empty stool, right next to Tyge. Quietly and on a hunch, he said, "I hear you're in a tight spot."

Tyge tensed, cut a glance his way, then relaxed his white-knuckled grip on his beer. "Someone been talking? Malone, maybe?"

Pretending ignorance, Cade asked, "Is she someone I need to chat with about this?"

"Nothing she can tell you."

"Who can, LaMonte? You?"

The other man hunched his shoulders. "Nothing to tell. And, even if there was, ain't none of your business."

"Well, now, being that you're a member of the association and I'm a director of same, I'm afraid it would be my business."

Tyge turned to face him. "What do you want, Delaney?"

"I want you to keep your nose clean and stay away from Malone."

"So, it was her. Should've known. No loyalty anywhere anymore."

"Really?" Fury ripped through Cade. Quiet, deadly fury. "How many times has she taken you back when your luck and your money ran out? A half-dozen? A dozen? And, with losers like you, the luck always runs out, isn't that right?" Cade had seen it too many times. Despite the strides the sport had made, he supposed there would always be one breed of rodeo cowboys who drifted from one woman to the next, eating their food, sleeping in their bed until they either made enough at the pay window to move on or got kicked out, only to do it all over again with the next.

Tyge snarled and got to his feet. "I did for Malone what you wouldn't do. I helped her make her dream and I helped her live it. Yeah, man, I screwed up plenty and I lost her. But you screwed up first. You lost her first. Now, keep the hell away from me."

Despite the sucker punch of truth, Cade stood firm. "I'm serious, Tyge. Stay away from Malone. You're not going to use her again. If you're down on your luck, find yourself a hole to crawl into but not anyplace near her."

"Hell, a man can't even have a drink in peace." Tyge threw a twenty on the bar and headed for the door.

Cade squelched the urge to follow him. His foremost thought as he got in his truck was that Malone was not going to be happy with his interference.

* * *

Huh. There's plenty of bustle around the barn even in this late hour, but it seems an unusual time for play. And I might add I've always found this particular human-canine pastime unintelligible. The Aussie, trembling with anxious anticipation, waits for his master to throw some kind of stick—not a run-of-the-mill chunk of wood, mind you, but a carved stick made to look like a large bone— so that he can race to retrieve it, only to have it thrown again.

I've a feeling the location of their game, within viewing distance of

Malone's rig, is no coincidence. We moved her truck and trailer from its earlier check-in location to a place with hook-ups for plumbing and electricity. Much nicer than the din of the generator, though that is probably very useful when she's traveling cross-country. Numerous security lights hold the dark at bay. The horses are all snug inside the barn area with its entrance to the climate-controlled arena where, last I checked, Malone hand-walked each of her very large horses in turn. That all made me more than a little nervous for her safety. Too many other contestants were astride and cantering, those well-muscled legs and sharp hooves passing right beside Malone. Some of those animals weren't all that well-behaved. Not in my opinion anyway.

It seemed to make Joss just as nervous. She hovered at Malone's side, moving quickly to place herself between her mentor and approaching riders as much as possible. Malone noticed the protective movement just as I did. I could tell by her half-smile each time the young girl changed positions.

I spy Joss walking out of the large building now. I suspect that means the horses are settled and Malone is on her way. I watch for her and she soon emerges from the barn in conversation with the young man who has had an eye for Joss though Joss wants nothing to do with him or with any human male creature. I'm sad for her that her experiences at the hands of some of them have not been good. She's been left with a deep mistrust, but she seems to understand that Cade, at least, is not a threat to her.

She's a pretty girl and I've watched her play with Malone's face products some evenings, but she washes the color enhancements away at bedtime and never wears any outside of the living quarters of the trailer. It may be years before she trusts the normal things of life that most girls her age are able to take for granted.

Townie has grown fond of her and on his next fetch races toward her with the stick rather than returning it to Cade. Her face lights up with a smile as she accepts the wooden piece, which has to be repulsively damp by now.

As interesting as it is to see these humans at work and play, repetition grows old. Still, boring as it may get, keeping an eye on things is all just part of tending to humans.

It took me a time or two to figure out what Dax seemed to sense in me from the very beginning of our association. I'm good at figuring things out. I have a strong sense of fair play. I'm relentless in making sure the innocent are protected and the guilty are made to pay.

Now, while my current humans are all accounted for and in close quarters to one another, I should have time to take a turn about the grounds. There may be information out there that needs to be gathered, maybe even hints of criminal activity waiting to be revealed or a mystery to be solved. Even if that doesn't prove the case, I'm sure I won't learn anything of consequence by loitering here.

Although this is not my first rodeo—pun intended!—I've only recently come to understand that professional rodeo is a very nomadic existence. I'm sure most of the contestants gathered in this place have a home base, just as Malone does, but it seems the more successful of them don't get to spend much time there.

The barn and the outbuildings are still lively and I pick my path with caution. I don't much like the idea of being trampled or of stepping into some disgusting pile of droppings. Townie might relish the opportunity to roll in some nastiness, but that's a dog for you.

Not all of the activity around me is horse-related. I pass a boy chatting up a girl and then what looks to be a young couple in a heated disagreement. Not too far past them, a pair of half-grown males engage in some serious roughhousing. It's all in fun now but could end in a bruise here and there. None of which is any business of mine.

I pause near a small gathering of cowboys who stare into a pen of muscular horses with shiny coats and point out which are most rank to one another. As best I can tell from their conversation, I don't think rank used in this regard means either a foul smell or a rating of some kind. Further along, the bull riders are involved in much the same stance and conversation as they gaze at bulky animals with wicked, long horns. The eyes of the bulls are as bright as that of the broncs but with a glint that seems, at least to me, to contain a clear 'ride at your own risk' dare.

I'm about to give up snooping, at least for this evening, when I hear voices around the corner of the next small building that carry a darker undertone, not anger but not idle chitchat either. I edge closer, keeping to the shadows, so as not to be noticed. It may already have become apparent to some that Malone is traveling with a very intelligent gray cat and I'd rather remain inconspicuous for now.

It comes as no real surprise that the discussion proves to be about money. My experience with humans has given me a pretty good understanding that money—or its lack—is at the bottom of many human shortcomings, frequently resulting in the failure of friendships, business partnerships, and marriages.

Something about the voice of one of these two catches my attention and I move closer. Unfortunately, I still can't see them, can't study their faces or expressions, unless I round that corner and risk exposure. I don't think that's my best course of action. Not just yet.

"You owe me for the last job. I need the money and I want it now."

"You'll get it after the next job. I promise. And a bonus with it. My word on that."

"Your word?" *That snarl speaks volumes.* "There won't be a next job. Not for me. I told you I'm out and I mean it."

"There is no 'out' for any of us. You knew that walking in to this."

"The hell I did. You changed the game and the rules halfway through the last load. If you'd been anywhere around when I found out what I was hauling, I swear to God, you wouldn't be standing here, now, running your mouth. Forget it. And forget me."

"You're making a mistake, cowboy. A dangerous one. This isn't a game and the rules are what they are, when they are. You need to remember, I'm not the one calling the shots and I'm not the one you're going to answer to when you don't show up at the next load point." *A wealth of menace is carried in those words and that tone. The cowboy he threatens—whoever he is—should probably watch his back. It's his voice that nags at me, but I'm not sure why that is.*

"I won't be there. Tell your boss and you can also tell him that his little enterprise won't last long if gofers like you keep pulling tricks on drivers, like you did with me."

A soft laugh conveys anything but humor. "You still don't get it. It wasn't me who pulled the trick, as you call it, and you aren't the first sap to get dragged deeper into the spider web. All I do is tell losers like you where to be and when to be there. I'm curious about something though … what pulled you out of hiding?" *He chuckles as if he knew the answer before he asked the question.* "You went to ground and then you show up here. What's the draw, cowboy? Did I push the right button?"

"You can go to hell."

The voice is farther away and I'm guessing this conversation is over. For now, anyway. I really need to get a glimpse of these men, though. And I need figure out which is which. But, as I slip around the corner, both are walking away, angled in different directions. The shadows, which provide great cover for me, don't allow me to see much in turn. I can tell only that both are similar in build, average height and slim-hipped with broad shoulders. Both wear jeans and boots and western hats as do about a hundred other men here. I could never identify them in a lineup. Only their voices will distinguish them to me and I can only hope to encounter them again.

With all that said, I have no means of knowing if this exchange has anything to do with the deputy marshal's investigation. I didn't hear any real proof of wrongdoing, but my suspicions are strong that's just what they were discussing. To be honest, my goal seems a bit murky for now. My concern for Malone began with a glimpse of jeans and boots disappearing into her trailer without her knowledge. But Joss isn't a threat and doesn't seem to carry any threat with her. The girl is afraid of recognition, that much I'm sure, but we're far from Lake Charles, Louisiana. Beyond that, it's not likely anyone searching for her could've trailed her through our crisscrossing of the country. Her arrival seems nothing more than a coincidence and that is the needle that jabs at me. I don't trust coincidences and I never have.

And while it's true, there's an investigation into some sort of crime in or around the association to which Malone belongs, it doesn't seem to involve her, even on a peripheral or happenstance level.

The only hint of trouble surrounding her seems to be linked to the telephone calls from her former boyfriend, who seems to have gotten himself in a bind with some less than reputable business partners. And then it hits me. The voice on the speaker phone with Malone! That was the hint of familiarity in the conversation I just overheard! And, as they would say in some cheap novel, the plot thickens. Was Malone's cell phone number the 'right button pushed'? Had the threat of danger to her drawn the cowboy from his safe hiding place?

Oh, the frustrations of not being able to concisely communicate all that I know to the right human, in this case Cade. I'll find a way as I always do, but I'll need the right moment, the right opportunity … as with the cell phone. In the meantime, I've got plenty to keep me busy if I'm to figure out just what's going on while keeping Malone and Joss safe at the same time.

Chapter 8

Malone leaned against the railing of the warmup pen where she and Callahan watched Joss long-trot one of the horses Malone had placed in her charge. Joss had proven herself a tireless worker with a gentle but firm hand on a horse. Barrel racing and rodeo were new to her, but she was a fast and willing learner. She'd confided to Malone that she preferred her new surroundings to the roughness of the horse track, but Malone knew both sports had their seamier side.

Joss had seen the more sordid aspects of horse racing before finding herself in the upper ranks of rodeo. But there could be no *upper* anything without an equivalent *lower*. Malone would protect Joss from that if she could.

Not that Joss considered herself in need of protection.

In fact, in the past day or two, Malone had felt herself shepherded between Callahan and Joss so that she was never alone. The fact intrigued her as much as it perplexed her.

A soft sound from Callahan had Malone turning. She hadn't yet deciphered all of his sounds and signals but knew he was as good as any watchdog when it came to letting her know she had company. She smiled a greeting as a man stepped closer and propped his arms on the railing beside her.

"Brax, how are you? I saw Luke last night. He said y'all are holding fifth place in rankings. That's wonderful."

Brax and his son, Luke, had more than enough earnings to secure them a spot in the circuit finals, as her own winnings had done for her. She liked the duo and was always pleased to see them. She hoped they'd do well here and that they'd make the association finals at the end of the year.

Malone didn't see a need to mention to Luke's dad that their conversation centered more around Joss and his son's attraction to the girl. The questions he'd asked about her had been aimed at determining her age and whether or not she had a boyfriend.

Brax smiled at her. "We've had good year. I enjoyed roping with my older boys, but I'll tell you, my Luke, he's something else. I taught him everything I know and now I'm learning from him. A seventeen-year-old. Go figure."

Malone chuckled and turned her attention back to Joss who was swinging out of the saddle and walking their way, leading the horse. Joss gave Brax a questioning look and Malone fought the urge to roll her eyes as she made introductions, including the fact that Brax was Luke's father. Surely that would reassure Joss as to his lack of threat.

Her introductions didn't include any particulars about Joss. Not only because she had so few—although Joss had admitted she would turn seventeen in January—but mainly to keep her safe.

Only a little reassured by the introduction and Callahan's lack of alarm at the visitor, Joss moved off to hand walk the horse around the pen a few times. Because the animal was in no need of cooling out, Malone realized Joss had no intention of leaving Malone on her own with this man while she returned to the barn for the next horse on her list to ride.

"I heard you might be relocating, changing circuits next year." Brax's voice held more than a hint of disappointment. "What's prompting that?"

"If I make the change, it will be earnings, plain and simple, but I haven't made any final decision. For now, I'm competing in both, spending most of my time in Oklahoma, Texas, Arkansas, and Louisiana where some really nice payouts seem to be in clusters. Our circuit has some of the largest single payouts," she admitted, "but the distances in between are greater and I've had some prospects open up for me in the Southeast that I don't have farther west." Malone had made a name for herself through sheer hard work. Because of that, she'd been offered horses to ride that were out of her price range to purchase. She'd leave her current home base in Oklahoma with a pinch at her heart, but she had no family to speak of and friends in nearly every state from Georgia to California. "If I do, it will be a business decision." And, perhaps, the pull of her grandparents' home which was still alive with her happiest childhood memories.

Brax removed his hat and rubbed his ear. It was a gesture she'd seen him make when he was thinking hard about something. "Means I'll only see you once or twice a year unless I can persuade you to some other opportunities."

Malone shook her head and smiled. They'd had this conversation more than once.

"Damn, woman, you're a hard one. Can I take you to dinner tonight, to celebrate both of us making the finals again this year?"

With a rueful smile of friendship, Malone turned him down, as she had in the past, but his quick grin and the shake of his head said he'd be asking again.

As he walked away, she found Joss looking from him to her. "He's a nice-looking guy for an older man. Why won't you go out with him?"

"His wife died three years ago. He's lonely and looking for a replacement. I'm not it."

Joss snorted. "From the way he was looking at you, he doesn't see you as a 'replacement' for anyone. He sees you for you."

"Maybe. But I'm not interested in a relationship. They don't work for me."

Joss turned to lead the horse back to the gate and barn. "*One* didn't work for you," she tossed over her shoulder. "Doesn't mean all of them won't."

Malone didn't bother to correct her. Besides, she couldn't really call her past with Cade a relationship. They'd been best friends, she'd *thought* once, and moving slightly toward something more, she'd *hoped* once. Anyway, what she'd gone through with Tyge, before and since their breakup, was more than enough to keep her unattached.

She was amazingly happy and darn well planned to keep it that way.

And though she didn't say it, Malone also felt a bit pleased that whatever bad things had happened to Joss hadn't turned her against men and relationships, at least if they didn't involve her. Joss continued to keep her distance from Luke, but Malone couldn't blame her for that, something very bad had brought her into Malone's world and not that long ago. The bruises were fading and all but gone, but the memories would likely last a lifetime. Malone knew she wasn't trained or equipped to give the girl the expert help and advice Joss needed, but she was wise enough to know that, for now, Joss was in a good place here with her, simply feeling safe and welcome. And, again for now, that would have to be enough.

* * *

Cade worked in his office as long as he could stand it. Tonight was the first go-round for the competitors. Excitement was running high and tension was running higher and the noise level in the business office had ramped up right along with it.

Grabbing his hat, he stepped into the open area behind the counter, saw a line of contestants, each of whom would have a different question, a different need that should have been asked, identified, and resolved much earlier than this morning. People were people and some would always leave things to the last minute. Even important things. Cade sighed and looked around for his right-hand administrator.

Aleta grinned and rolled her eyes when she caught sight of him. "Escaping?"

"Maybe for a little while. Everything under control?" It damned sure didn't look like it.

"Yes, believe it or not."

Letting some of his tension ease away, Cade headed through the glass door on the customer side of the counter. Aleta would have let him know if she needed him to stay or intervene with anyone or anything. He greeted several contestants by name on his way out but didn't slow for a chat with anyone. Even Townsend seemed to be in a hurry to escape the building as he matched Cade step for step.

The wind was an unexpected slap in the face. It had risen since the pre-dawn hours when he'd stepped into his office. But the breaking sunshine was a welcome sight. He knew he'd be dragging by the end of the day, but sometime around three o'clock that morning his mind and the worries it contained had awakened him. Although he'd done everything he knew to ensure this event was a success, he'd taken a risk in moving the location of the first title round. Failure wasn't an option, but success wasn't a given. That left him somewhere between *this had been a sound decision* and *what the hell had he been thinking*.

Although he didn't have a destination in mind, Cade was hoping to run across Malone and wish her well for her run tonight. She was a skillful rider with talented horses. He wasn't sure which of them she would be astride for this first of six go-rounds, but he knew she would have each of those six runs plotted and planned. The ground would be as perfect as the arena crew could make it, but barrel racing in and of itself held danger. A horse could slip or stumble or spook. Fans who were also competitors would know and hold their breath, start to finish. Fans who weren't, would see the splash and sparkle of tack and wardrobe, and think it all a wonderful show. Which it undoubtedly was. Cade hoped the spills and thrills stayed with the rough stock riders, who expected, trained, and prepared themselves for it even as they hoped to avoid it with their skill and their luck.

The thought of seeing Malone, even if only briefly, had Cade whistling lightly as he strolled around the corner of the bronc holding pen.

* * *

For Pete's sake, whoever Pete is, what is it with these male humans? Can this punk not see that Joss isn't interested in his attentions? I'm not sensing a real threat from him, but he needs to move along. I just hope I don't find it necessary to intervene but, if she gets any more uncomfortable, I'll have to toss my hat into the ring and remind him of his manners.

"Come on, honey, pull that old thing off your head and let's see that pretty hair. I'm betting with all that green in those eyes of yours, you're a true blonde, right? Or maybe a redhead. I'm partial to redheads."

Does he actually think that grin and wink are disarming the object of his attentions? She's growing more and more tense, backing away from him, but she's reversing herself into a corner and hasn't realized that, very literally, her back will soon be against a wall. And, as he takes another step toward her, she takes yet another step back.

Darn. Looks as if it will be necessary for me to intervene.

"Back off, jackass!"

I turn as does Joss's tormentor to see an admirer of a different sort leaping over the fence railing to get to her. I recognize Luke, whose attentions have been nothing but polite and admiring toward

Joss these past few days.

"Get lost, Roberts. Busy here, in case you didn't notice."

And isn't this just dandy with the two kids facing off for a fistfight and Joss looking like she wants to lose her lunch.

"Walker." *The tone of Luke's voice gives fair warning.* "I mean it. Leave her alone."

"I don't see no ring on her finger or through her nose."

"You also don't seem to see that she wants to be left alone."

Walker shrugs and turns his back on Luke, making it clear he doesn't see Luke as any real threat. He smirks at Joss. "That right, sweetheart? You really don't want to let me see what color your hair is under that old hat?" *He takes another step closer.*

And that's all it's going to take, it seems. Luke's hand reaches out and spins the other young man around. Luke doesn't land the first punch as Walker comes around swinging and connects solidly with a cheekbone. But Luke does land the second, and if that crunch isn't a broken nose, I'll be surprised.

I look across at Joss. Her face is ashen and devoid of any expression which is more than enough for me. Time to take matters in hand. With my usual strength and speed—which I'll admit sometimes surprises even me—I leap into the fight, finding a solid landing spot on Walker's shoulders. His build resembles that of a young, strong bull and so does his current state of fury. I sink my claws deep in warning. He makes a grab for me, but I don't fear for myself so much as for Luke who definitely doesn't have the killer instinct I sense in Walker.

"What in the *hell* is going on here?"

Perfect. I recognize that booming voice. Cade has arrived on the scene and Townsend with him. The dog is growling with a menace the opposite of his normal peacefulness. There just might be more to the canine than I thought. If the fury in Cade's voice is any indication, he'll soon have this matter in hand. Thank goodness the two have sense enough to respond to the tone of authority and drop their hands to their sides before another punch is thrown.

While Cade sorts through the fight, I'll see to a very shaken Joss.

* * *

Cade looked from one battered face to the other. He recognized both of them. "Either of you care to answer my question?"

"He was upsetting Joss," Luke finally answered.

"Bullshit!" Walker glared and rubbed at his shoulder where Callahan's claws had been buried. Blood trickled from his busted nose. "I was just flirting, just having a little fun with a good-looking girl."

Townsend growled again and Cade spoke quietly to him. Townsend reluctantly sat at Cade's heels, ready to enter the fray if allowed.

"Fun at her expense, you jerk. Didn't you even care about the look on her face! She didn't want you to pull her cap off."

At Luke's words, Cade glanced at Joss and the fury that had begun to subside churned again. Cade pulled out his cell phone and started making phone calls, his hard glare daring either combatant to take a step in any direction. The first call was to Malone and all he said was, "Joss needs you," telling her where to find them. The second call was to Luke's dad. He hesitated on the third call, looking at Walker. "You're one of Nick's hands, aren't you? Roland Walker?" He got a sullen nod in response and placed the third call.

When Brax and Nick arrived within moments of each

other, he told all of them not to go far because he had things to say and decisions to make. Then he focused on Malone who came into sight at a sprint, taking in the scene, putting Joss behind her protectively, and turning her glare from one battered face to the other just as Cade had done. But her gaze held as much disappointment as anger when it settled on Luke who looked down at his boots.

Cade walked over to Malone and spoke softly. "I'm sorry this happened. I'll deal with it and check on Joss as quick as I can."

Malone hesitated, very much looking as if she'd like to throw some punches herself. Cade had no doubt she'd make them count. Fortunately for all, like Cade, she knew that wasn't what Joss needed from her.

Cade was surprised when Callahan, after glancing from him to Malone, chose to stay behind as Malone put her arm around Joss's shoulder and steered her away. Maybe the cat wasn't done with Mr. Walker either.

After a brusque, "Come with me," Cade led the way back to the show office, leaving Nick and Walker in the waiting area while he spoke privately with Luke and his dad in his office.

Callahan perched upon a window ledge behind the desk, while his Aussie took point midway between the desk and the door, sitting at attention as if ready for anything untoward. Cade didn't expect that, but then he hadn't expected to come upon Joss looking ill while two of his members swung fists at one another either.

Looking across his desk at the two of them seated in the most uncomfortable chairs he'd ever seen, Cade knew he had a hard decision to make and he wasn't entirely sure what he was going to do. He frowned at Luke. "You know the rules about fighting, about physical violence of any kind."

"Yes, sir."

Brax scowled and opened his mouth as if to protest or defend his son, then closed it again. He knew Luke faced expulsion which would put an end to both of their hopes and dreams for these circuit finals as well as the association finals later, for this year and indefinitely into the future.

Cade was glad Brax held his peace and let the boy make his own path through an unpleasant and potentially devastating set of circumstances. The simple, quiet response impressed Cade. Luke wasn't going to make any excuses for himself. Nor was he going to apologize for coming to Joss's aid.

Callahan appeared equally impressed. He leapt from the window sill where he had positioned himself upon entering and walked to sit down beside Luke. He met Cade's glance and Cade almost felt reprimanded. At the least he felt challenged. He repressed the smile that wanted to emerge. The cat's antics and perceived judgement on events might be entertaining, but the situation they were in was anything but a smiling matter.

"I gathered from your comments earlier that your intent was to protect Joss from Walker's unwanted attentions. You happened on a situation you didn't create and you reacted to it."

Luke hunched his shoulders and said again, "Yes, sir," adding, "I didn't throw the first punch, but only because he beat me to it." He looked up and met Cade's gaze evenly. "I would have. I wanted to hit him. I wanted to hit him, and I would have."

Brax hung his head at his son's admission.

"Fair enough." Cade leaned back in his seat. "Ever been in trouble before, Luke. School? Anywhere?"

"No, sir."

Again, Brax looked like he wanted to speak and Cade decided to give him that chance. "You got anything you want to say?"

Brax sighed. "I taught my boy to take up for himself and for others. I won't fault him for what he did and I won't blame you for what you need to do. But I will say this to you and anyone else, Luke's a good kid, no trouble— just like he told you. God's truth on that. He's a straight A student and works harder every day after school and all summer than half the men on my payroll." He looked at his son. "And I want *him* to know that I'm proud of him, right here, right now, for coming to that girl's aid. Damned proud."

"I am, too." Cade said it so softly that it took a moment with both of them for the words to sink in.

Luke's head jerked up. "I can compete?"

"You can compete. Rules are rules for a reason, though, so you'll pay a fine. One hundred dollars of your money, not your dad's."

"Thank you, Mr. Delaney." Though Luke didn't smile, relief shone in his eyes and his shoulders no longer looked as if they bore the weight of the world.

Cade stood and walked with them to the door, shaking Brax's hand before he opened it. As they walked out, he gestured for Nick and Walker to come in. He didn't miss the dark look that Walker aimed at Luke.

Cade rubbed the back of his neck as the two took the same seats across from his desk. Nick looked disgusted, but Walker's expression was plain pissed-off.

Walker was likely only a few years older than Luke, but he was hardened by work and experience. Cade planned to be fair to both but took a different approach with Walker than with Luke. "Tell me what happened, Roland."

"That punk roper threatened me."

Cade kept his expression neutral. "Why would he do that?"

"Reckon he's got the hots for that girl works for Ms. Malone. Didn't like me flirting with her."

"Was she enjoying your flirtation?"

"Huh," Walker seemed to sense a trap and stalled for time. "What do you mean?"

"Just what I asked. Was she enjoying your attention, smiling at you, flirting back?"

"What did that little jackass tell you when he and his dad were in here?"

Walker's tone had turned belligerent. Callahan hissed. Townsend made a throaty sound that was not quite, but almost, a growl.

"Shut up, Roland, and answer the question." Nick looked furious.

Walker hunched his shoulder. "Maybe she would have if Roberts had stayed out of it."

"And maybe she wouldn't have. What then?"

"Aw, hell." Walker leaned back in his chair, crossed his arms over his chest. His glare made it plain that he didn't plan to answer any more of Cade's questions.

Cade looked at Nick. "You're an old friend. A good one. I won't tell you who to hire and who to fire. That's your call. But I will tell you to send this one back to the ranch if you plan to keep him on. I don't need him here."

Walker stood up before either of the older men had

a chance. "You're going to be sorry about this. I didn't do anything wrong. And that punk Luke's going to be sorry, too."

"Shut up, damn it." Nick's tone brooked no argument as he stood and slapped his hat on his head. He shook Cade's hand and thanked him. He placed a hard hand on Walker's shoulder, propelling him through the door that Cade held open for their exit.

Cade had that feeling of being watched and turned to find Callahan taking his measure. When the cat stood and stretched, Cade suspected he'd passed some kind of test.

Chapter 9

Malone tugged her western hat a bit snugger and took a deep breath. She fought the urge to dismount and check her girth or the wrap on the front boots. She'd checked both only moments ago. So much was riding on this moment, so much preparation and hard work for this talented gelding's owner, for Malone herself. They were as ready as they would ever be. Malone heard her name on the loudspeaker as being next up. Another deep breath and it was time to move into the alley. No time, no need to check anything. Time to go.

The gelding held tight in the turns, flicked his ears and listened to every quietly spoken request, heeded every light touch on the reins, every easy nudge of a booted heel. Malone marveled that, even with the stakes this high, she was relaxed … thinking and acting rather than reacting. It was a good run. She knew it before they reached and rounded the third barrel. Their time was going to be good, something to be proud of, and if she was blessed, something that would result in another paycheck.

She sensed rather than saw the cowboy step from the side of the alleyway just beyond the gate and, for a moment, her heart lifted and she felt like that teenaged girl again. But it wasn't Cade who reached up to put a steadying hand on the gelding's reins.

"Great run, Malone."

She sighed, irritated at her own disappointment, and swung down from the saddle. "I thought you were in hiding."

Tyge gave her a familiar lopsided grin that did nothing to hide the look of strain in his eyes. "Too much unfinished business."

For a long moment, Malone said nothing as she studied his face, the lines that hadn't been as deep the last time she'd seen him. She'd cared a lot for him once upon a time. A part of her would probably always care—at least a little. But that was a road she wouldn't travel again. "Just keep me out of it, okay?"

"That's what I'm trying to do, babe. I promise."

Malone turned to walk away.

"I need you to call me if anybody bothers you."

Swinging back on one heel, Malone felt an all-too-accustomed and very unwelcome rise of tension. "I have a feeling if you stay away from me, I won't have any problem."

Tyge looked at her a long moment. "If I thought that was true, you'd never have to lay eyes on me again. I swear to God. I need you to be careful. Please?"

Malone could feel his stare on her back as she led the gelding away. Joss caught up with her halfway to the barn, her face flushed with excitement and admiration. "You're holding the lead, Malone!"

Despite the exchange with Tyge, it wasn't as much effort as Malone thought it would be to smile at Joss's enthusiasm. "There's still a few more super nice horses to go," she cautioned but, still, it *had* been a really good run.

She ran her hand along the gelding's neck as she and Joss walked companionably. Malone crooned her pleasure to the horse and smiled her thanks to those she passed who congratulated her on having a fast, clean pattern.

"You have a lot of friends," Joss commented as they reached the barn.

"We're as much family as friends, I think. We compete in the same circuit, spend a lot of time on the road together. If I need a helping hand, there's always someone to lend that. If somebody needs me, I stop what I'm doing and help where I can."

"But you're competing against each other."

Malone chuckled. "Not really. Not most of us. We're competing against the clock. I'm never out to beat any other barrel racer, just always trying to beat my own last performance."

Joss fell silent and Malone supposed she'd given the girl food for thought. Going for casual, she said, "I didn't get to watch the calf roping. How did Brax and Luke do, do you know?"

"Third, I think. That's still good, isn't it?"

Well, that answered her question. Joss had cared enough to watch Luke rope and enough to pay attention to the other times to figure out where he was sitting in the go-round. But all she said was, "Just *being* here is good. Pulling a check for third place is pretty fantastic."

They turned a corner in the barn and Cade straightened from his comfortable prop against the stall, Callahan and Townsend at his feet. Malone felt that lift again and fought to quell it.

"Nice job." Simple words.

Malone smiled. "Thanks."

"Should I unsaddle?" The hint of impatience in Joss's tone made Malone wonder how long she and Cade had been standing there staring at each other.

"I've got this," Malone said. "Why don't you start getting ready for the reception?"

Joss frowned at her. "I'm not going."

"Of course, you are. All of the contestants and their families go." Malone had thought Joss was adapting to the family atmosphere of the rodeo crowd and was dismayed at her refusal. Besides that, Joss would be better with her than alone in the trailer half the night. When Joss's expression turned mulish, Malone tried tempting her. "Luke will be looking all over for you."

"I'm not a contestant or family."

"You're my family at the moment."

Malone was almost surprised when Cade broke in. "You'll be with the two of us, Joss. It will be fine. It's a fun event, food and a band and it only lasts a couple of hours. You'll enjoy yourself. I'll make sure of that."

And just like that, Malone realized, he'd paired them together. That didn't sit well with her, but now wasn't the time to argue the point. She wanted Joss to be comfortable enough to go with her. Besides, there was something in

Cade's tone that caught and turned her attention. She suspected he wanted to talk with her, most likely about this morning's incident.

Joss wavered, looking from one to the other. Her gaze came to rest on Malone. "I don't know what to wear."

Malone tilted her head and let her gaze travel the length of Joss's slight build. "Find some leggings or jeggings. There's a long emerald green sweater in one of the drawers or closets. You'll like it and it will look great on you. I'll be there soon."

As Joss turned to go, Malone noticed Callahan leave his cozy position in the stall shavings to follow. She thought he gave Cade's Australian Shepherd a supercilious look, but she had too much on her mind to dwell on that.

She tied the gelding and began untacking him. "What happened with Joss?" She had deliberately not asked the girl any questions and Joss wasn't ready yet to talk about it.

Cade sighed as he lifted the saddle from the gelding's back. "A punk cowboy messed with her some. Wanted to see her hair and apparently got a little obnoxious in his insistence."

"Apparently?" Malone fought to keep hold of her temper.

"Either that or Luke over reacted. When I got there, they were taking swings at each other. A couple of them connected. Joss was pretty shaken up but not harmed."

"Who is he?"

Cade laughed softly. "And at the end of that question, I hear the unspoken death threat."

Malone laid her forehead against the gelding's warm neck. That was exactly what she was feeling, but she didn't say so. She felt Cade touch her hair.

"I'm almost sorry I can't turn you loose on him. He's one of Nick's hands. I told Nick to get him off the grounds and out of here. It didn't matter if he fired him or sent him back to the ranch, but he wasn't working the event."

She stepped back. That should have prompted Cade to drop his hand, but he twined his fingers in her hair and tugged gently until she moved closer. For a moment, just one brief moment, she let herself lean against his chest. With a deep breath, she straightened and said, "Go away, Cade. This isn't going to happen."

"It just did," he told her softly before he let her go.

She wouldn't let herself watch him walk away. But she wanted to.

* * *

It'd be helpful if I had more information, a lot more. Instead, this is how it always starts … with nothing, and I put next-to-nothing together with next-to-nothing-more. The puzzle begins to take shape. The answers become clear. It's what I do and I do it well.

But a starting point is helpful and usually elusive. Unfortunately, this time, I have more than one, and they appear to be unrelated. As much as I enjoy the tempting layout of food, I'm going take this opportunity while competitors and rodeo staff are entertained to nose about a bit. But one last visit to the statuesque brunette manning the spread of roasted meats wouldn't be out of line. And isn't that an interesting spin of words. Why did humans not coin the word 'womanning' when describing a female who makes things happen the way they're supposed to?

And, see there, proof of my point. The lady has already noticed me though my approach is unobtrusive. She lifts a plate and begins arranging the best pieces, nothing dry, nothing unappealingly spiced.

Neither barbeque nor hot sauce hold any appeal and she's careful that nothing of the kind touches my plate. When it's full, she places it on the floor beneath the table at her feet. I don't have to fear being trampled while I eat. Hers is the most popular table, though I'm not certain if that's because of the prime rib or succulent pork roast or the fact that she's not hard to look at.

Maybe she treats every repeat customer with the same care as she has me. That would be explanation enough.

Licking the plate clean, I head for the chill of the night. Of course, I have to wait at one of the entrances until it opens to a pair of fancily booted feet. I exit and move toward the less traveled, business end of the facilities where stock contractors load and unload their prized animals.

I've given a lot of thought to Deputy Marshal Ryder's conversation with Cade. He implied that more than horses and cattle were being moved from place to place by some elements of the rodeo world. From the news I've watched with Dax, drug and gun traffic from Mexico is known to be heavy along the corridors that cross the lower United States. We're central to that here, but certain addictions are thriving throughout all of the continental states. Those drugs have to reach far-flung places by some means. What better method than the ever-popular rodeo which has found a place in nearly every state, if memory serves—as mine always does.

A cat never knows what might be learned when humans are otherwise occupied. The scent of drugs is different from the smell of food. Humans have trained dogs to perform tasks like drug detection, but that's only because they've learned felines won't do tricks for them. It did cross my mind to bring Townie along but only for a moment. He's nice enough and more intelligent than most. But he's clumsy and this situation calls for stealth.

I'll do much better on my own.

* * *

Cade walked into the open area that had been set up for the opening night reception. The outer perimeter was framed by at least a dozen tables each draped in black linen and covered with appetizers, meats, seafood, vegetables, or bread. Aleta had outdone herself and he noted with amusement that the meat tables outnumbered the remaining tables by half. Wise woman.

The DJ played a familiar country artist at an acceptable sound level, but no one had taken to the dance floor. He knew they might not. Most cowboys needed more than a couple of drinks before braving the dance floor and, though Aleta had made sure to have a good offering of high-class beer and wine available, he knew there'd be only moderate alcohol consumption tonight. This was a highly motivated group of competitors and their focus this week wasn't hard partying. Still, they would all welcome the show of appreciation for their hard work and support of this association that the reception was intended to convey.

As his gaze swept the room, Cade didn't try to pretend to himself that he was doing anything but looking for one brown-haired, brown-eyed drum runner. He'd missed her for so many years the sense of loss had turned into a dull ache, which he'd pushed to the back of his mind and heart while he earned a living in the sport that he loved, vacationed in places most people only dreamed of, and drifted through several long-term relationships that never quite went anywhere.

He now knew why they hadn't and why none ever would. Having Malone at the back of his mind had only meant she was deeply rooted and always there. He finally, fully accepted she always would be and he was determined to get it right this time. His only hope was that she wouldn't prove just as determined to deny him that chance. Malone was one hard-headed cowgirl.

It was her hair, the rich shimmer of what should have been *just brown*, that caught his attention and pulled his gaze to her. Her back was to him and her shoulders were squared for a fight and it was Nick Andrews she had in her line of sight. Cade started their way.

Nick looked as miserable as any real gentleman would be as he tried to fend off the fury of her comments. Cade heard a few of her castigations as he got closer. He understood her distress, but he also understood that an employer couldn't necessarily screen on personality traits. Some, like Nick and other stock contractors, had to focus on knowledge of livestock and physical ability as well as a willingness to work long, hard hours in temperature extremes from sweltering summer to winters of ice. Sometimes that came with honesty and integrity and a well-mannered disposition and sometimes it didn't.

Walker had acted like a jackass, but—in all honesty— he hadn't done anything seriously wrong, just obnoxious. He had no way of knowing Joss's history made her a poor choice for his clumsy effort at flirtation.

Nick saw him coming and his eyes widened with relief. "Cade."

Malone turned at the sound of his name and Cade gave her a quick, appreciative glance. She'd traded jeans and boots for a long turquoise tunic of some sort, belted at the waist, over leggings that—while they looked warm— also looked sexy as hell. Although she said his name in greeting, he couldn't tell if she was glad to see him. It was plain she was much too angry with Nick at the moment for any other consideration.

"Malone, all I can tell you is I'm sorry and there won't be any more trouble from Roland. I sent him back to the ranch. I sent him to the hotel right after it happened, told him to pack his bag and hit the road at first light."

"You should've fired him."

Nick rubbed his brow. "Now, Malone, I can't fire every cowboy that acts stupid over a pretty girl. I wouldn't have anyone left to work for me except a few old timers who learned their lessons a long time ago and most the hard way. Roland acted stupid, but he didn't mean any harm."

Cade suspected Nick wasn't going to get far with that argument, and he was right.

"Well, you'd better figure out a way to keep the rest of them in line. If you can't teach them a girl's no means no, then I'll make them understand."

"I ain't their mama or their daddy and they should've learned that lesson a long time ago, but I'll have that talk with the rest of them."

Cade wanted to snort at the image, but one look at Malone's chin made him rethink that urge. Nick beat a hasty retreat, and Malone tracked his departure with a steely gaze.

"Stupid," she muttered.

"Hey," Cade said softly. When she turned to look at him, he was pleased to see her temper fade.

"Hey, yourself."

"Where's Joss?"

"She wouldn't come with me."

So that was what had her so furious. Not just the incident but that it had set Joss back a step or two on trusting the people around her. "I'm sorry, Malone," and he was, "but Nick wouldn't have had that happen for the world."

"I know, but darn it, Walker isn't a teenager. He's a grown man and Joss is a kid. He could see that as well as anyone. I want to pound some sense into his head."

"And Joss is more fragile than most girls her age in similar situations. She has a history Walker doesn't know about."

"I'm not sure he would've acted any better if he did," she said darkly.

Cade couldn't argue the point. He wasn't sure of that either.

From the loudspeaker, he heard the tempo of the music shift. The dance floor was still empty but, on impulse, Cade took a risk—a big risk—and swept Malone into a cowboy waltz. For a moment, she stayed stiff in his arms though her feet instinctively found rhythm with the music.

When he murmured in her ear, "I've wanted to do this since the wedding at Summer Valley Ranch," Malone relaxed into the dance and Cade found himself grateful to the long-ago girlfriend who had talked him into taking lessons with her.

Glancing down at the curve of her cheek, Cade felt a contentment he hadn't known in too many years. He had no intention of giving that up, not without a fight.

With a final slow spin as the music faded, he stopped them at edge of the dance floor and nudged Malone so that her gaze followed his. Joss stood near the doorway, looking very pretty in green, but also looking shy and a bit uncertain. Her hand was grasped by Luke who didn't look unsure in the least. Apparently, he'd done what Malone hadn't been able to do and convinced Joss to join the fun.

Chapter 10

The back of the facility is no less well-appointed than what the fans see from their box office seats surrounding the competition arena. It's well-lit and properly maintained with stout railings for the livestock that it shelters. Unlike the highly trained athletes of the barrel racers and ropers and steer wrestlers, these animals are bedded down in small herds. They are no less bright-eyed and healthy than their four-legged counterparts but definitely not as pampered with separate lodgings.

I'm forced to admit that it does look as if serious effort has been given to cleanliness. Even with that, there's no denying the odor of droppings picked up and placed in bins around the pens. That gives rise to the likelihood that even the odor of illicit drugs might remain undetected in this area. At least to the uneducated.

The first animals I pass are what the rodeo announcer called the broncs, though I cannot distinguish the saddle broncs from the bareback broncs. The next are bulls with massive horns. As fierce as they look, their manner is peaceful—at least with one another. The only restive group is the last, the young bovine for the calf-roping event. I can't at first see the cause for their fretful behavior and circle closer. They could just be hungry and anxious to be fed. But there's hay in multiple racks along the railing.

Plenty of hay, fresh water, no predators. I guess it's their youth that prevents them from settling. With a little maturity they'll come to understand and appreciate the value of a good night's rest.

Not a hint—or a scent—of illegal narcotics, but I won't say I've wasted my time although my efforts haven't produced one thing of concern.

As I turn to go, I catch a glint, a suggestion of something shiny, not in the pen but on the other side, closer to the block wall at the rear of the building. I circle around to investigate even though it doesn't appear large enough to be of significance. I'm bored. I admit it.

As I get closer, a faint but unpleasant odor tugs at me. The glint that caught my eye turns out to be an abandoned spur—nothing fancy to it—a small swirl of black filigree inlay on the side, but much the same as I've seen on the competitors. It's just your garden-variety, blunt-ended spur with a leather strap worn through. Some cowboy or cowgirl will be missing that soon, I think, but I don't turn back. The smell has become stronger and all-prevailing. Slowly, I realize the odor of droppings hid more than the possibility of unlawful trafficking. They covered the scent of death, one still so faint that humans wouldn't likely be able to detect it. Yet.

I follow the airborne trail around a corner and find the body propped upright between two beams. There's no sign of a struggle but, as I tell myself, the guy didn't break his own neck, that's for sure. I check to ensure the presence of an intact spur on each boot and make a mental note of the lone, abandoned one as possible evidence.

I sure hope Luke has a good alibi as his altercation with the *deceased got a lot of attention. Time to find Cade and make known the death of young Roland Walker.*

* * *

Malone preferred not to acknowledge, even to herself, the sparkle of awareness that zinged through her every time her glance met Cade's, which seemed to happen way too often. They'd danced, sure, and it had been nice—more than nice—but she'd *been there, done that* with him and didn't plan for a repeat even though they were two very different people now. And that—the differences—was part of the point. Her life had moved on from Cade and it confused her that he wanted to revisit a past that had been so hurtful, at least for her. She never thought of herself as a coward. She'd taken on and won some of life's hardest challenges. She'd carved success and happiness out of what sometimes felt like solid rock. But, even with all that, some things took more courage than even she could boast.

Cade's popularity as director had given her easy opportunity to put distance between them and she'd taken advantage of the fact. She found a glass of water and carried it as a buffer between herself and any other offers to hit the dance floor. Although she had no problem telling the cowboys no—she'd done it for years—it softened the refusal to claim thirst and a need to catch her breath, as if she'd been dancing every dance. She wondered sometimes why they continued to ask at every opportunity.

As she chatted in a corner with long-time friends, a glimpse of gray fur caught her attention and she gave a second look. Callahan wove his way through denim and leather. There was intensity to his movement that caught her eye. She reminded herself he was always just that focused in his hunt for food he thought worthy of him. She would have thought, though, that he would've had plenty earlier. When it became clear he was bee-lined for Cade, she excused herself from the conversation and made her way back across the room. Odd as it seemed, she was beginning to pay attention to the cat.

Callahan reached Cade seconds ahead of her. He stretched upward and placed his paws on Cade's jeans. Deep in conversation with one of his staff, Cade idly rubbed the cat's ears and found himself swatted for his effort.

Malone smiled despite herself. "Come on, Callahan, I'll go see."

Cade glanced her way, then back at Callahan. Malone was surprised by the look of acceptance in Cade's expression. It seemed they were both coming around to Callahan's influence. "Why don't you wait here and I'll check out what's bothering him?"

"Nope. He's with me … although he seems to have forgotten that at the moment."

After a quick look around the room reassured her that Joss was well occupied on the dance floor with Luke, Malone turned and walked to where her jacket hung from one of the many coat racks placed near the door. She wasn't surprised when Cade's Australian Shepherd met them there. She'd witnessed that, even when the dog appeared to be in solid slumber, if his master moved, he knew it.

Callahan led the way out of the warmth and music and into the beauty of the night. The wind had died with the onset of dusk and stars had overtaken the sky. It was cold, but not bitterly so.

Her pulse leapt as the streak of gray took them toward the barns, then settled as Callahan bypassed where the competitors' horses were stalled. She felt Cade's occasional glance her way, but neither had spoken since leaving the reception hall.

They passed the bucking stock and Callahan slowed his pace. For the first time Malone felt a slight sense of dread. Something was very wrong, but she couldn't have said for sure how she knew that. They could be following the cat on a wild goose chase … but she didn't think so. She wished for a flashlight. The barn wasn't in complete darkness, but the few lights that burned high along the walls weren't enough.

Callahan sat in the middle of the hall and looked up at them with a sound somewhere between growl and rumble. When he had their attention, he batted at a spur barely discernible in the dark. Cade hesitated. It could belong to anyone. Competitors lost equipment every day, a broken hook, a broken strap were common mishaps. He'd likely never find the owner. Still. He picked it up and slipped it into his back pocket.

Blinking, Callahan stood and led them around another corner.

Malone felt shock hit the back of her throat in the form of nausea and she swallowed hard. Cade said the ugliest word she'd ever heard him utter before pulling her into him so that the young man's body with its grotesquely twisted neck was hidden from her sight.

* * *

Cade made a calculated decision and hoped it wasn't

a wrong one. The first call he made wasn't 911, it was to Deputy Marshal Ryder. 911 was next. His third call was to Nick Andrews.

While he waited for the authorities to arrive, he hit Aleta's number.

"What's up, boss?" he could hear the surprise in her voice.

"I need a favor, more than one."

"Sure."

"Wrap things up and get everyone out the door as soon as you can. Tell them I hope they all rest well and wake ready for a successful round two." He checked his watch. "It's only a quarter of an hour early so hopefully no one will question."

"I'm questioning."

"You question everything," he reminded. "I'll answer as I always do—but later. I also need you to make sure the girl traveling with Malone gets to their trailer safely. Make sure she locks herself in, and tell her Malone will be there soon."

"Something bad has happened, hasn't it?" Aleta's voice held gloomy resignation.

"Yeah."

"What else, boss?"

Beside him Malone's teeth chattered, though he suspected that was due more to shock than cold. "See if you can scrape up a thermos of coffee or two. All hell is fixing to break out here and we're going to have plenty of company."

He told her where they were and smiled faintly as she said, "On that, boss."

Because it had been nearly time to close the festivities

for the night, anyway, he hoped he might get lucky enough that some contestants didn't hear about the death until morning. The police had been asked to come in the back entrance of the facility without lights and sirens. He'd emphasized the need to avoid panicking the livestock, but not being surrounded by a several dozen contestants and event workers would be a definite benefit.

* * *

I didn't appreciate nearly enough the efficiencies of Cade's assistant. That was my bad. The redhead arrived not only with two flasks of coffee, she also brought a small cup of cream, with the chill removed, for me. Even Townie was not forgotten, his tail wagging energetically at the beefsteak bone she carried wrapped in a napkin.

Malone cradles the coffee in her hands for warmth but seems frozen in place and doesn't drink. I can sympathize. I remember my own first glimpse of violent death. It left a nasty feeling that was not easy to shake.

Although I don't think Cade is immune, he remains stoic as he orchestrates the comings and goings of various entities, giving directions, providing information as needed, and making phone calls when requested. Periodically, he turns his gaze on Malone. Whatever he's thinking remains unspoken.

An ambulance is backed with care into the narrow opening not too far from where the body, now strapped to a gurney, awaits transport. Pictures have been taken from every conceivable angle. Surfaces have been dusted for fingerprints and I've no doubt a multitude will be found, with none relevant to the case. This wasn't a clumsy deed done in a fit of rage. It takes skill to deliberately break a human neck. Skill and a cold-bloodedness that not many humans possess. But there are benefits. It's quick. It leaves little trail. There's no murder weapon to discard. There's no blood which could be carried away in tell-tale sign.

Cade places a hand on the shoulder of his friend Nick Andrews who looks as if he's been gut-punched. As Walker's employer, and with no family present, he signs the paper on the clipboard that is handed him by the ambulance driver.

As the ambulance pulls away and the rollup door of the barn area is lowered once more, an officer walks up to Cade. "I'll need to speak with a Mr. Roberts now."

So at least one of the hangers-on who drifted in has told a tale out of class. I sigh. Humans rarely realize the ill effects of their gossip.

"Which one?" *Cade's voice carries the edge of his irritation.*

"Luke Roberts."

"Aleta, would you ask Luke and his father to come to my office? We'll join them there."

"I don't need his father," *the officer protests.*

"Luke is seventeen. You won't talk to him unless his father allows. Or I can go ahead and call an attorney now." *There is steel in Cade's tone though he has been nothing but polite until now.*

The officer yields with a nod and we all troop back to the show office building. Cade places his arm around Malone. She doesn't lean against him, but she neither does she push away. I flank them on one side, Townie on the other. I'll admit the dog continues to display limited uses ... very limited.

Minutes later we're all crowded into one small space. Aleta quietly closes the door on us. To my surprise, though the officer glares around the room once as if counting heads, he doesn't ask anyone to leave. At Cade's discreet nod, Luke's father has agreed his son can answer a few questions. I understand Cade's reasoning. It's often these preliminary forays that set the tone for the real investigation. That twisted neck is the work of a cold-blooded—and likely professional—killer. The sooner the authorities realize that Luke doesn't fit the bill, the sooner they'll direct their effort in a better direction.

The officer flips open his notepad and begins asking questions any decent mystery writer could have crafted. Dax and I have watched enough mystery movies for me to know the right questions are being asked. Why had Luke and the deceased traded blows earlier in the day? Had they known each other previously? When was the last time Luke saw the deceased? Where was Luke during the two hours prior to the body being found?

With his father's hand resting lightly upon his shoulder, Luke acquits himself well, remaining quiet-spoken and polite and without hesitation in his responses. His youth comes through as surely as the unlikelihood that he had the skill or the bulk or the sheer ugliness of nature it had taken to break Walker's neck, much less the time. He'd been with his father or friends during a timeline he was able to recount without hesitation. The only response that draws even a hint of consternation from the officer is when Luke told of being with Joss, talking her into attending the reception and escorting her there.

He glances around in resignation. "I suppose this Joss is also seventeen."

"Sixteen," *Malone says,* "and asleep." *I see the quick look she exchanges with Cade and surmise her concern. If questioned by the authorities, Joss may well disappear in a panic.*

The officer closes his writing pad at last and looks around. "I'll expect to have all of you here and available for any additional questions in the days to come. And Ms. Joss as well."

I peek around the corner of the door as he exits and am not in the least surprised to see the ever-efficient Aleta hand him a thermos and what looks to be two nicely wrapped sandwiches to take on his way. His surprise turns to gratitude and I note the lines of weariness on his face as he thanks her.

Cade sends the Roberts, father and son, off to get some rest then nods to his assistant. "You can show Ryder in now."

"Thank God." There is a wealth of feeling in those two words. I gather the deputy marshal hasn't been the most patient of visitors.

Ah, well, one down and one to go.

* * *

Ryder glared at Cade. "What does that mean? The cat found the body? I asked what you and Ms. Summers were doing, both of you dressed for the festivities you abandoned, strolling through the barns where a dead guy just happened to be?"

"We weren't strolling," Cade said patiently. "We were following Callahan. I told you, he came to get us."

"Bullshit."

The urge to grin took Cade by surprise. Nothing funny about death and even less about murder, but Ryder's expression was priceless. Cade suspected the other man was more than a little irritated that he'd had to wait his turn to grill Cade and Malone. He wasn't on the scene officially. He was there because Cade had been cooperative enough to call him. He owed Cade that, plus the spur with the leather strap which could prove to be worth something or nothing at all. Callahan had seemed to think it was evidence of something. Cade wasn't convinced either way.

Ryder looked from Cade to Malone and back again before his gaze flicked to the gray cat in the windowsill.

"You think this dead guy has something to do with my investigation?"

"I don't know if it does or not. You asked me to call

you if I saw anything I didn't like. I damned sure don't like what I saw in that barn." Cade could feel Malone's gaze on him and knew she'd be demanding explanations of her own as soon as they were alone.

"So, you don't think this Walker was killed because of a fight over a girl? That's what was being hinted out there among some of the other contestants."

"I have no idea why he was killed, but I'm confident Luke Roberts wasn't who broke his neck."

Malone straightened at that. "Luke didn't kill anyone. He's a good kid."

"But he punched the daylights of out the guy earlier today."

These were all questions they'd already answered. Multiple times. The answers weren't going to change with retelling. Cade stretched his back and shoulders and rolled his neck, trying to relieve some of the tension. It was hours past midnight after an already long day. He knew Malone must be exhausted.

He got to his feet, forcing Ryder to do the same. "Look, I've told you everything I know. Just like I told the police everything I know. Now I'm going to ask you to go do your job and let me do mine, which has very little to do with a murder investigation."

Chapter 11

Malone opened her eyes and froze. Joss! It was full daylight and she was alone in the trailer. Well, not quite. Callahan sat at the foot of the bed where she'd collapsed, fully dressed, too few hours ago.

She let herself relax. The cat had proven a good barometer. Joss was someplace safe and Malone had horses to tend. She glanced at the clock, relieved that it was still very early and that she felt more rested than she would have thought.

Minutes later, dressed for the morning chill, she opened the door to her living quarters. Joss rose from one of the two canvas folding chairs she'd placed close to the door. She handed Malone a thermos and a sandwich. Her large, expressive eyes were troubled. "Horses are fed. I hand-walked Diablo, but he's going to need to be rode."

"We'll ride everyone lightly except Jaz. I'll hand-walk her."

She unwrapped the sandwich, bit into warm bacon, cheese, and egg wrapped in a light pastry crust, and nearly moaned with pleasure. Most of the time she cooked in her tiny kitchenette, but this was a welcome treat and time was valuable, considering how much of the morning she'd lost. Although, it appeared Joss had made up for that on her behalf.

Because Callahan didn't bat an eye as she savored her food, she knew he'd been happy with his breakfast. He'd probably had two of the wraps to her one.

"How did you decide who you're going to ride in the finals?"

"Contestants don't decide. Where we are in year-end earnings make the decision on whether we ride and who we run, if we compete on more than one. But I wasn't surprised when Jaz made it in this year. She's the best I've had. Ever. Diablo almost squeezed in because he can handle just about any ground although he skims across the top of fresh dirt easier than some of the others who like to dig deep. Scamp just needs more time. He'll be right there with Jazz and Diablo someday. The other three are going to be solid money-earners but maybe not up to this level. Fortunately, their owners are more into jackpot runs which are a lot of fun and still bring in money enough to keep going. Rodeo is a different intensity." An intensity that she'd loved as long as she could remember.

She finished her breakfast wrap and opened the thermos, sighing with real pleasure at the deep, rich aroma of it. Not coffee. A latte. "Thank you for this."

Joss shook her head. "Not me. Luke brought it." She hesitated then added in a rush, "He didn't kill that guy."

"Of course, he didn't."

The teen's shoulders relaxed visibly and Malone studied her over the rim of the thermos. "All of this is going to be okay, Joss. It's truly ugly and I feel more than bad for Roland Walker's family, but the police will figure it out." She hesitated. "But I'll need you to be careful until they do, okay? Stay close to me and keep the trailer locked when you're inside alone."

Joss looked at her with those young-old eyes and Malone remembered she was talking to a girl who'd probably seen things that would make Malone shudder. She *hoped* that one day Joss would trust enough to share. What she *feared* was that one day Joss would disappear as soundlessly as she had landed in Malone's life. Still, she was Malone's to protect for now.

Callahan accompanied them to the barn where things were busy for the next few hours. Malone was pleased to realize that Joss no longer ducked and turned away when acquaintances stopped to speak with them.

After one such exchange, as they rode two of the horses at a quiet walk, side-by-side, Joss said, "You're popular."

"I've been around longer than many and made a lot of friends." A few enemies, too, she acknowledged to herself, but it had never been intentional.

"The really little blonde on the really big roan, that's who beat your time last night, isn't it?"

"Yep. She's ridden that mare to the finals three years in a row. They're an awesome duo."

"But …?"

Malone chuckled. "But nothing as far as the competitor

or the competition here goes. Courtney works as hard as anyone I know and gives everything she's got every time and she's friendly, always willing to extend a helping hand. Still, it would scare me to have everything pinned to one horse. She's got a couple of three-year-olds she started hauling this year, and they're showing promise, but she keeps them on the back burner. The others she competed on this year are loaners that she's barely ridden."

"She seemed a little snooty to me. I was watching everybody when you were warming up. When the other girls tried to talk with her, she would cut them off and move her horse away."

"Most of that is nerves. You'll find a lot of competitors want to be alone with their horse right before a run. It helps them focus. Others would rather be distracted with conversation. Courtney is really very friendly, not snobbish at all. But she gets tense when the stakes are higher and the circuit finals are almost as high as it gets."

"I don't care. I still hate she had the fastest time."

Malone laughed and shook her head. "No single competitor is going to pull first place at all six goes here. I've never seen it done in any of the events. I'm not done, Joss, no worries."

As she eased the horse beneath her to a canter, she was aware when Joss headed back to the barn for her next mount. She felt pleased she hadn't even had to tell the girl what the horse had needed in pace and duration of this morning's ride. Joss was picking up more and more regarding the animals Malone had entrusted to her.

For a little while Malone was able to shake off the nightmare of the murder, but as she slowed Diablo to a trot then a walk, she felt as if a gaze was fixed on her. She glanced around, but all she saw were fellow competitors, walking, talking or otherwise focused on their own tasks at hand. No one who appeared interested, much less overly interested, in her.

Still, the feeling stayed and she wasn't surprised to find Tyge waiting for her when she led the untacked gelding into his stall. A bit unnerved, perhaps, but not surprised.

Tyge rose from a crouched position in the corner of the stall and moved to the opening as she maneuvered the muscular horse around him. So, he wasn't afraid to be seen. But when she gave him a searching glance, she could see that his eyes were shadowed. Haunted, even.

"What have you done?"

"I didn't kill Walker."

She sighed. "I know that." And she did. Just as she knew Luke had not. Tyge skated the line on respectability, but there was no meanness to him. There never had been. She slipped the halter off and watched as Diablo shook vigorously then moved to his hay bag. Too many thoughts crowded her mind.

"But you're involved. Somehow." She didn't make it a question and he didn't answer.

"Not with murder. That's not me, Malone."

Wordlessly, she picked up the bucket that held Diablo's grooming gear and brushed past Tyge. He moved out of her way while she secured the stall door.

When he fell into step beside her, she whirled on him in exasperation. "What do you want from me, Tyge? You called me in a panic, warning me to be careful, begging me not to tell some nameless someone where you were. Then you're here in the wide open and not hiding at all. And a man is murdered. Murdered! What the *hell* is going on?"

Instead of rising, her voice had gotten lower and lower with the apprehension that held her in its grip, so low the last few words had to be forced past the constriction in her throat.

Tyge put both hands on her shoulders and, for one brief moment, she saw a different man, a man who'd once been front and center in her world, caring about her hopes and her ambitions as much as he'd cared about his own. And he'd had them. Tyge was going to be a world champion. He had the skill and the physical ability and the mental determination. And he'd been close, so close. Malone had respected that man, shared her dreams with him, trusted her future to him.

That trust had long since turned to dust and been swept away with the wind.

For a moment, she thought he'd turn and walk away. As he'd always done before. That was Tyge. Take the easiest way out.

He surprised her when he didn't. "Sometimes a man has to be more than he thinks he can be. More than the woman he loves thought he ever could be. I'm in trouble. I'll admit that. And I don't want you dragged in to it. I'm here to make sure that doesn't happen. I didn't kill Walker. He wasn't a threat to me. But I'd kill for you, Malone."

She felt no warmth at his declaration. She couldn't be moved by words of caring from him. Not anymore. Not ever again. Particularly when coupled with mention of murder. Instead, ice touched her spine. Tyge wasn't loquacious or eloquent. If he bothered to speak, it was with intent. Something bad was going on around him and he'd brought it close to her and to Joss.

Frustration made her feel harsh and the harshness was

reflected in her tone. "Maybe if you disappeared again, any threat to me would disappear as well."

"If I believed that, Malone, I'd make it happen, no matter how much money they owe me."

Money. She tried not to think of all the things that could be tied to money and murder.

She took a deliberate step back and Tyge's hands dropped from her shoulders. His look of regret spoke volumes. But it wasn't enough. Not nearly.

As he turned away, she sighed and shook her head. She had things to do and no time to worry over things she couldn't control.

She started forward but was stopped in her tracks as the large gray cat stepped into her path. She'd been so intent on her exchange with Tyge, she hadn't been aware of Callahan's arrival. He swung his golden gaze from her to Tyge's retreating figure and back again.

Callahan growled softly and she said, "Yeah, me, too. I don't like it one bit, but there's not a damn thing I can do."

* * *

Huh, I take that to mean she has no intention of sharing this exchange with Cade. That would be a serious mistake. Sure, I understand not getting the cops involved. I get the impression she feels some loyalty to this character. Besides, she's got nothing concrete to offer. And I don't imagine Cade has anything either, and I don't think he'd be any more able to solve this mystery. What I do think is that each has different pieces of the puzzle. They should work as a team to fit those pieces together for the final analysis. I've noticed people, unlike cats, don't always act in their own best interest. Case in point.

I don't like what I know so far. There's a very real threat to Malone, and the danger is tied to this Tyge who is tied to the man who got his neck broken. Or, more ominously, the person who broke it for him. Joss's unexpected arrival on the scene, which is what brought about my involvement in the lives of these people, appears to be nothing but a twist of fate and, yet, there's something that warns me not to trust happenstance.

My senses are on hyper-alert, but I believe Malone is safe for now. It's daylight and Joss is unusually watchful for a young girl. Which is, no doubt, due to whatever brought her our way to begin with. If I hope to learn much of anything, it looks as if I'd better follow along with Tyge.

The air feels better this morning, crisp and clear without the wind clawing at my fur. More like what I want, and expect, on a nice autumn day. Which reminds me that winter isn't all that far away and that's not my favorite season. The cold doesn't bother me, but the wet days of rain and sleet aren't fun for any activity except taking a nap. Dax isn't the napping type so I don't see much of that in my future now that we're traveling companions.

I can't be sure just yet, but Tyge seems to be ambling with no direction in mind. And the layout of the structure is well suited to that. Whoever designed this barn may have had a method to his madness, but I can't see it. The twists and turns are that of a rabbit warren.

In the same moment I realize we have circled the same space over again, I comprehend that Tyge's gaze is searching and far more keen and intent than his ambling steps would imply. It may be that his goal is to 'accidently' cross paths with someone. I'm not happy with myself that I didn't pay attention sooner to more than his boots dawdling along.

Tyge hesitates then moves purposefully toward a cowboy who wears jangling spurs and a belt buckle that—as they say—is bigger than Texas. The cowboy moseys just ahead, a cell phone to his ear. Mosey is a nice cowboy word I heard on one of our Dirty Harry videos. It's a nice little nugget to add to my vocabulary.

Tyge takes advantage of the cowboy's inattention. With hand to shoulder, he spins him about with a sharp aggression and the phone goes flying from the other man's hand.

"You owe me."

No pretty words from Tyge this morning, at least not for anyone but Malone.

"Only thing you got comin' to you is an ass-whooping."

Tyge bristles like a cur dog at those words. "You want to try, asshole? Go ahead." *No one's fool, but equally no one's picture of a gentleman, Tyge doesn't wait for the first punch to be thrown after issuing the challenge. And he makes his first punch count. The cowboy with the jangling spurs staggers and puts a hand to a nose that's no doubt as broken as it is bloody.*

"You bastard."

"Yeah," *Tyge taunts,* "that's me, a son of a bitch of a son of a bitch. But quit whining and bring it."

Unfortunately, it appears the cowboy will have help 'bringing it'. Without warning, there are two additional pairs of hands, one on either side, holding Tyge immobile as the cowboy swaggers close.

Fortunately, Tyge has two things in his favor. He has shown a tenderness for Malone, which has to—and does—carry weight with me. Added to that, I have an affinity for evenness, even in a brawl. Three to one is not even. Adding another won't even things out but will sure bring it closer, especially since that other is me.

My leap, quick as ever, lands me squarely against a thick neck. I dig my claws into a meaty shoulder and close sharp teeth on a vulnerable ear. The bellow the thug emits sounds a whole lot like that of one of the rodeo bulls as it exits the chutes with an unwanted rider on his back. As thug one spins in confusion, I make the leap for thug two. I'm disappointed when I miss my intended point of landing on the shoulder. My claws dig for purchase through hair that is greasy and in need of a good soaping. The squall that erupts is every bit as satisfying, as I sink claws into the equally unwashed scalp.

I spring gracefully to the top of a wooden railing and watch Tyge take good advantage of the pain and confusion I handed out. He wades in with both fists flying and soon gives both of us the pleasure of seeing all three punks on the run.

I'm disappointed when Tyge doesn't give me any credit for my quick-thinking intervention as he stands there with abrasions that are bad but not as bad as could have been. He sneers at their flight then turns away, somewhat unsteady from their treatment of him, but on his feet. I don't get a thank you or even a glance of appreciation.

All I can do is remind myself I didn't intervene for Tyge as much as I did for Malone's sake. Still, I can't help but feel insulted and disappointed in Tyge as I stalk away in search of Cade. Maybe he's found something more important than saving an ungrateful wretch from a beating he probably deserved!

Chapter 12

"I want to put an undercover agent on your staff."

Cade's instinctive thought was an abrupt refusal, but he tempered his words to Ryder because the man had a job to do and Cade respected that. "I don't have a place or a function for anyone. My team would be suspicious."

A car whizzed by and Cade snapped his fingers to bring Townsend a bit closer to heel. They were on the sidewalk between the perimeter of the expansive grounds and the streets of the city. Very busy streets.

When Ryder had called at an early hour, Cade agreed to meet but away from his office. The deputy marshal could no more hide his military bearing than Townsend could shed his canine nature. Walker's death had left everyone on edge and Cade needed their attention focused on the event and not the investigation that swirled around them. Distraction made for mistakes and mistakes made for failure and sometimes injuries and even death. The contestants had worked too hard to get here for them to meet with inefficiencies in the event itself.

"Deputy Armand is twenty-eight years old and looks ten years younger. She's been around horses all her life. You'll introduce her with intentional vagueness as some veterinary student who is kin to one of the city officials. You've just been advised she's always given part-time work at any equine events this large. She'll take care of the rest of her disguise and her investigation."

"You want me to lie to my team."

"Damn it, Delaney. You've had one dead body here. You're just as likely to have another. But those are the bad guys and I'm not real concerned with their wellbeing. So, yeah, I want you to lie to your team if it will help me nail the guilty and protect the innocent."

Cade rubbed the back of his neck, feeling the pressure of what he was being asked to do, stacked up with the pressure inherent to directing an event that was the culmination of a year-long effort for the finalists. He and his team were dedicated to ensuring the event itself created no hardships that might hinder the drive of their members for success. But Ryder was asking him to help with something that could put a murderer behind bars and more. Ryder's investigation couldn't prevent, but it might at least slow the distribution of drugs and the untold suffering that came with that distribution. And if it were guns rather than drugs, the stakes were even higher.

Hell. "Alright. Send her."

His phone buzzed in his pocket. Aleta. Hopefully

not with a problem. He turned away from Ryder as he answered.

Aleta went straight to the point. "There's a plain-clothes officer here. I verified his credentials. He's in your office." He heard the hesitation in her voice as she added "He's got Malone Summers penned up in there, apparently planning to grill her pretty hard. He asked me to wait about thirty minutes before calling you to meet with him."

Good for her. "Thank you for not waiting. I'm on my way." All sides of law enforcement were on the job early today. He turned back toward the show grounds and Ryder fell into step with him.

"Problem?"

"Nothing unforeseen. Our local investigating officer has shown up."

Ryder grinned unexpectedly. "He wouldn't be happy to see me here. The locals get a bit touchy about jurisdiction."

"Aren't you going to need any information he can gather?"

"Not much for him to find, is there? No weapon, so nothing to find there, not even potential fingerprints. Possible DNA under the victim's fingernails, if he had a chance to fight, but nothing to match it with. Even so, yeah, I'll want to see what he comes up with, but desk jockeys can deal with transfer of information. I'll be on my way for now, but I'll be in touch." When they reached the parking area, the marshal simply stepped away between the rows of massive trucks and trailers.

Cade wondered wryly if the man had intended that last comment to be reassuring. It was anything but. Cade supposed he could add juggling two opposing law enforcement agencies to his tension level.

Keeping his stride long but easy, Cade made his way across the grounds, threading through and greeting contestants and staff but not stopping. He wondered if any of the familiar faces hid secrets that would come to light in the next few days. It sickened him to think that people he knew and trusted might be involved in something as bad as drug or gun running. He prayed it wouldn't come to that, but he'd help expose them if it did.

Aleta gave him a concerned look as he stepped behind the counter of the outer office. Seeing her distress, he gave her a slight nod and a reassuring wink. He didn't feel the least surprised when Callahan stood from a curled position on the counter and muttered at him.

Without hesitation, he opened his office door and stepped through, focusing on Malone's expression and ignoring that of the plainclothesman who stood as he entered. "You'll need to give us a while here."

Cade tamped down his anger at Malone's haunted look and said, "You're in my office." He kept his voice easy but added, "Uninvited." He held out his hand, "Cade Delaney, Director of Operations for Twin Circuit Rodeos."

The officer squared his shoulders and pulled in his slight paunch as he shook Cade's hand but retained his officious expression. "Detective Marchmann."

Careful to keep the lead, Cade invited him to be seated, gesturing to the other side of his desk. He was pleased to see that the detective, who looked to be near retirement age, wouldn't stand out in any crowd, medium height, average weight, ordinary features. His shirt and slacks were neat but not crisply tailored. He'd blend in anywhere, a typical Joe.

"What can we help you with?" He aligned himself

with Malone and allowed himself a sideways glance at her. Although her lips were no longer compressed into thin lines, she hadn't relaxed into her chair but kept the same faultless posture with which she sat a horse.

Marchmann sighed. "I was just having Ms. Summers walk me through finding the body."

"For the third time."

Cade swung his gaze to her and kept it there a moment. There was the faintest hint of humor in her eyes and that relieved him. He turned back to Marchmann. "And did you learn anything different during the second and third round?"

"You don't want to interfere in this investigation." Marchmann added a scowl to his words.

"You're right. I don't. A young man who should have been safe in this city is dead. I've got rodeo grounds full of contestants who should feel safe at this facility and now they don't. When the city council approached me about moving this event from Little Rock to Montgomery, I was assured this was becoming one of the safest cities in the south. I expect your department to be quick and efficient in making an arrest."

"Even if that person is associated with your organization?" Marchmann jabbed.

Cade pierced him with a deadly cold look. "Especially if."

As if sensing he'd met his match and even been slightly bested, Marchmann took the seat he'd been offered, not even bothering to ask Malone to leave when he told Cade, "I'll need your statement and as much as you can recall of last night's events."

"Certainly." And Cade talked him through every aspect

of the evening except the moments he'd waltzed with Malone, holding her close as he'd once given up all hope of doing.

Marchmann had fewer follow-up questions than Cade expected. Either his own observations from the previous night had filled in any gaps that Malone's had left or their memories were so aligned, the detective couldn't find any gaps to close.

He looked dissatisfied but resigned when he closed his notebook and put away his pen. "I need to talk with Luke Roberts and, yeah, I know his father needs to be present. Maybe the girl, too. I don't have her name but the one that witnessed the two fighting."

Cade got to his feet. He had no intention of allowing Joss to be questioned, but he'd fight that battle if and when it came to that. "I'll have my assistant contact the Roberts' and bring you some coffee. Feel free to wait here. It may take a few minutes for her to get in touch with them."

As a surprised Marchmann murmured his appreciation for the offer of coffee, Cade stepped around his desk and held out a hand to Malone who took it and rose gracefully from her chair.

When he opened the door, Cade noted that Townsend moved to stand beside him, but Callahan simply stared at Cade and blinked. Apparently, the cat preferred to sit and listen to the next exchange. For a moment, Cade's total acceptance of Callahan's unique characteristics struck him with amazement then he mentally shrugged. He couldn't ignore what he'd observed and experienced with the cat so far.

He glanced at his watch. Barely lunch but close enough. With any luck, he'd convince Malone of that. As they walked out into the reception area, he said her name before she could slip away and she turned to look at him. "A minute?" The hesitation in her eyes was evident, but she nodded and stayed close to the outer door while he spoke with Aleta.

"Marchmann wants to talk with Luke. I'll need you to call Brax to bring Luke over to meet with him here. I told Marchmann I'd make sure he got some coffee so I'd appreciate your help with that. Make it a full carafe."

Aleta nodded. "Why don't I send someone to the deli to pick up lunch for all three of them?"

"That's a good idea. Do you have someone you can spare?"

At her nod, he said, "Get enough for you and your team, then. Maybe a few platters of cookies to set out for any of the contestants who drop by this afternoon."

His assistant was smiling as she turned away. The stream of contestants with requests—some urgent, some petty—sometimes seemed never-ending. Cade knew his staff would be more than appreciative of the lunch as a small gesture of thanks for their patience and something as simple as an offer of a cookie could take the edge off a contestant's irritation over a complaint.

He felt a little guilty that he'd withheld the agreement with Ryder. He'd let Deputy Armand settle into place before he told Aleta she was an undercover agent. Aleta's initial reaction to the arrival of an unexpected staff member would need to be as natural as possible in front of the others. He didn't suspect any of the office staff of wrongdoing, but he could take nothing for granted.

He didn't keep secrets from Aleta, but neither Marchmann nor Armand needed to know that. Aleta he would trust with his life and anything told to her in private would go with her to the grave.

He planned to tell Malone over lunch. If she would go with him. Big if.

Cade held the door open for Malone and she walked out into a day that seemed far too bright and beautiful. A man had been murdered in a violent, ruthless way. Somehow it felt wrong that the sun was shining and the air crisp and cool. Yesterday's overcast sky would feel more appropriate.

Cade was silent as they left the office, but when she angled toward her trailer and the next task on her mental list, he took her hand and tugged in the opposite direction. "I was going to the café a block over for some lunch. Come with me. Please?"

For a moment, she had that same swept away feeling as the evening before, when he'd taken her with him into a cowboy's waltz. Instinctively, she started to resist then thought, why should she? After all, they'd been best friends once upon a time. It wasn't inconceivable that they could be again. "Is it lunch already?" she asked, admitting to herself she might be stalling a bit. It had been so long ago, that time when friendship had turned to a crush, a silly school girl crush. She didn't know him now at all. And he didn't know her.

"I missed breakfast, so anywhere in between works for me." But the searching look in his gaze told her his thoughts weren't on food any more than hers were.

It could be a mistake, she knew, but she nodded and fell into step with him. Some clocks couldn't be turned back. And she wasn't nearly as brave as the young girl Cade had known so long ago. But she *was* content and at peace, a hard-won peace at that. Even more, her life, everything about it, made her happy. Would she be willing to risk that? Maybe not, but neither was she quite ready to reject the possibility of a friendship she'd missed.

The walk to the café was short. Cade signaled his beautiful Australian Shepherd to wait outside the door as they went inside.

When he pulled out a chair for her, Malone felt uncomfortable and almost wished she hadn't come with him.

Cade seemed to sense her shift in mood and smiled at her. "Relax. It's just lunch."

"This feels awkward to me."

"It doesn't have to be."

"We're not the same people."

"Thank God for that."

His fervent comment drew a soft laugh from her that caught her by surprise and some of her tension slipped away.

"Were we really as bad as all that?" she asked.

He smiled. "You were hardheaded as hell and I was arrogant as hell. So, yeah, pretty much we were."

The arrival of a waitress to take their order provided a brief interruption and was just long enough for Malone to decide not to evade the conversation.

"I wanted you to believe in me," she said softly.

Cade leaned forward, resting his forearm on the table. She wasn't sure how eyes the color of a frozen lake could hold so much heat. "Malone, I did believe in you. You were bright and talented. I didn't doubt you could do anything you set your mind to, but you were only seventeen and there were so many possibilities in front of you. I wanted those possibilities for you."

"You never said."

"No. I said all the wrong things." He checked them off one finger at a time. "You were too young. You were acting like a brat. You didn't know what you were doing. You were dumb as dirt to walk away from a full scholarship, that rodeo would be waiting."

"Seventeen-year-olds aren't known for their patience. I didn't want rodeo to be waiting for me. I wanted it right then, right there. So, I went after it." With Tyge. And left Cade far behind. She was sorry for going with Tyge but not for going after what she wanted. This life had been good to her.

Cade leaned back in his chair, some of the intensity leaving his expression. "And maybe you were right to go."

His admission surprised her and she wasn't quite ready to explore what he meant by the words. "Grandma knew I was leaving. I don't know how she suspected and I don't know if she told Grandpa. She came into my room while I was packing what little I took and gave me two hundred dollars. Probably that week's grocery money. I was just selfish enough to take it."

"She would've been heartbroken if you hadn't. And your grandpa knew. He was the one who told me not to go after you … that the time wasn't right for us then, maybe someday but not then. He said if I went after you as angry as I was, I'd break the bond we had. Possibly forever."

The revelation stunned her. "I never knew you and he had even talked about me leaving … about us." The *us* that had never really been.

"He was disappointed in some regard, but he was proud of you, too. Said you were strong and knew your own mind. Told me to let you go until you were ready to come back."

But she never had.

She shied from that thought, from the look on Cade's face. "I always felt bad, afraid that my dad would blame them for not keeping closer watch on me that summer. If he ever figured out they'd known and let it happen, he would've gone on a rampage. And I missed them horribly." She'd missed Cade, too, but she wasn't ready to tell him that and knew she might never be. The first time she'd clocked a major win at a professional rodeo, she'd thought of Cade, longed to tell him. Not once had she considered he might be thinking of her too. And maybe he hadn't. Maybe he'd put thoughts of her aside until their paths had crossed on their upward climb through the world they both loved. But she wasn't going to ask him. Not yet. Maybe never.

It was almost a relief when their lunches were served.

Malone kept the conversation light as they ate and Cade followed her lead.

When they'd both declined the waitress' temptation of dessert, Cade paid the bill. "I'm glad you came with me. We said some things that needed to be said." He took her hand as she rose to stand beside him. "But not everything."

It sounded like a challenge, but she left that one alone. She knew some words were best left unspoken. "But now I have things to do and so do you."

"True. My event director is efficient but I don't like being away from the arena once the morning rounds start. This investigation has taken too much of my attention."

Malone felt a pinch of guilt as well because every competitor was expected to be at the arena when the colors were carried in, that event followed closely by the national anthem and the invocation. Even the fact that she'd been hemmed up by Detective Marchmann didn't dispel that sense of being somehow truant.

Only then, when they were halfway back to the grounds, did Malone recall the questions she should've been asking Cade during lunch.

"The marshal—Ryder—what is he investigating?"

"Murder, for one thing."

"And before the murder?"

"I'm surprised you let those questions go unanswered as long as you have," Cade admitted.

"Might be some of that patience you thought I'd never learn," she said lightly, even a little teasingly.

And, there, on the open city street, Cade did what he'd never really done, what she had longed for him to do all those years ago. He gathered her into his arms and he kissed her, long and hard and deep. And she really, truly wished he hadn't, for there went the friendship hypothesis. More than that, her response had been too swift, too intense, and way too obvious. At least to her.

Cade's release was as slow and reluctant as his embrace had been swift and urgent. He rested his forehead on hers and said, "It appears you gained what I lost. I meant to wait on that, to go slow and not scare you away."

Malone thought of all the things she could say in that moment, and all that left her lips was, "I'm not afraid." But she was also wiser than she'd once been, wise enough to know she needed time and space. "I'm also not forgetting the question I asked. What is Ryder investigating?"

When Cade told her, she was almost sorry she had asked.

"Drug smuggling? One of us?" As large as their organization was, most of them still considered one another family of sorts. The idea that someone she knew, someone she saw, rodeo after rodeo, and talked with as easily as she talked with Cade now, might be involved in something so vile was alien to her. Alien and abhorrent. As was the thought of a federal agent in their midst, posing as part of the staff and spying on them. "And Ryder thinks that's why Roland Walker was murdered?"

"I suspect it's a possibility in his mind, at least."

"Is it a possibility in yours?"

"I wish I could say no, but, yeah, a possibility … maybe even a probability. Ryder was already looking our way and he's suspicious enough to plant one of his team in my staff. Maybe it was coincidental that Walker happened to get his neck broke at the same time. I'm just not much into coincidences."

Chapter 13

That turned out to be a complete waste of my time. Detective Marchmann learned little of importance, if he learned anything at all. Since he didn't, I didn't. Not that I expected to gain much from the interrogation. I don't believe Luke had anything to do with a broken neck. But sometimes humans know more than they realize and a question or two from an expert can bring it to the forefront.

A hefty part of solving crime and catching criminals involves intuition and I have that in spades. Mine is telling me that Tyge's encounter with those thugs is linked to Walker's death. Yeah, sure, it's possible that there's more than one set of bad guys on the scene, but my mind doesn't lean in that direction. No, I think there's a link, and, if there is, I'll find it.

I'd like to question Tyge, but humans have real limits in understanding species other than their own. For now, I've gone too far and been gone too long from Malone and Joss.

***

Malone moved her bucket of brushes and combs and sprays to the next stall. Everyone got at least a half hour of grooming every day. Joss made it easier than it had ever been for her to give them that time and attention. The girl seemed tireless, constantly making rounds to clean and refill water buckets and scoop droppings from shavings to keep their stalls as clean as possible. Malone had told her, only half-joking, that she was going to have to find a gym to stay in shape if Joss kept doing the hardest work. Joss had just smiled and shook her head and kept going.

Callahan had joined her halfway through the grooming, moving languidly from stall to stall with her as she worked. With each relocation, he chose to sit upright in the open stall door, either careful to stay out from under sharp hooves or careful to sit where he could watch the hallway and the approach of any human. Malone wouldn't have bet against either probability.

As she ran a brush over a sleek red rump, she said a soft prayer for him as she did for each of them as she worked. Scamp was a quiet gelding, neither flashy nor fiery, so he rarely drew much attention outside of the arena, but inside, oh my, could that boy run and turn with a smoothness that deceived all but the timer. Malone wished again that he belonged to her, but then she wished all of them did. Scamp's real human partner was in her first pregnancy and had called Malone as soon as she'd seen the pink on the pregnancy strip. The amount she offered Malone to take him for a year had been generous and Malone had been honored by her trust in asking.

"We're going to surprise some people real soon, just you wait. There's more to you than they've seen. All I have to do is learn to stay out of your way." That was the hard part of riding so many different styles of horses. Some needed a little help, some needed a lot, and some—like Scamp— needed her to sit as quietly as possible and 'do no harm,' as it were. His one quirk was the last two or three strides of his run. If she wasn't careful to gather him up firmly at the right moment, he would express his exuberance at what he'd just done with a quick series of bucks before prancing from the arena. His owner had warned her and, so far, Malone had been careful to avoid any unwanted pitching.

As she worked, Malone listened to the announcer call names and times for the steer wrestling. There was a speaker in every barn and every warm-up pen so that contestants could gauge the various times they needed for each stage of their preparations as well as keep up with the successes of their friends and family. So many of the contestants were kin, father-son, brothers, mother-daughter, sisters. And some, not related by blood, felt more like family than those who were. Malone had fought with them and for them, knew them, loved them, despaired of them, but— yeah—so many of them were the family she didn't have.

Finishing her work, she decided to head back to the trailer to work some oil into another saddle and tack set. She'd done the same the day before. No two of the horses wore the same saddle and tack.

Halfway there, she was hailed from one of the practice pens and changed direction to talk with a long-time friend and competitor. Janie Grayson had started down the rodeo path a decade or two before Malone. Sidelined by a hip replacement, Janie was there for her daughter who was every bit as talented as her mother. These days Janie's primary role was to mentor and cheer on her daughter while keeping her two-year-old grandson out of the path of horses' hooves.

As Janie's daughter rode from the practice pen, she gave Malone a friendly wave. A pair of ropers rode past her into the pen. The team had been making a name for themselves the past year or two, moving up fast in the rankings. Janie scooped up her grandson and said her farewells, hurrying after her daughter. Malone stood a moment, admiring the fluid twists and turns of the horses in an unusual but effective warm-up pattern.

"Malone." She turned at the familiar, gravelly voice and smiled at Nick Andrews. He removed his hat in that polite way he had of always acknowledging the presence of a lady. It was old-fashioned and maybe even archaic, but she preferred that to having tobacco spit at her feet.

"Hi, Nick. How's it going?" She could see the shadows in his eyes and knew the death of one of his hands had hit him hard. Regardless of her opinion of Roland Walker as a man, he'd been Nick's employee.

"Could be better—especially if you'd accept a dinner date."

There was a twinkle in his eye that allowed her answer to come easily. "That answer's still a no, but the invitation is still regarded as a compliment."

"I'll keep trying, you know."

"I don't know why."

He gave a grunt of laughter.

She tilted her head to look at him. Nick was a good bit taller, with thick silver hair worn longer than was fashionable, a mustache the same shade, also longer than fashionable. Any sane woman would consider him a good-looking man and a catch with strong arms and shoulders and lean hips. She was just sane enough to appreciate the fact, but she'd never found herself interested in him that way and wasn't going to give him any hope that would change. And not for one minute had she ever really thought he wanted it to.

The sad truth was, after the failure of life with Tyge, she'd never found herself interested in any man that way, especially not with Cade always somewhere in the recesses of her mind to compare them to. And she was surprised that she was admitting as much, even to herself.

"Nick." She spoke his name on a sigh. "All these pretty ladies are giving you the eye everywhere you go. All you have to do is look around you."

"I don't want to look around." Blue eyes held a hint of sadness though he kept the slight curve of a smile on his lips.

Malone didn't kid herself that the sadness was on her account. Nick had never fallen out of love with his wife though she'd left him years ago. The death of their young daughter in the truck and trailer wreck that had put Nick in a hospital for several long months had devastated the woman. Nick had buried his grief in the stock-contracting business which kept him close to rodeo although he could no longer compete. His wife blamed the sport of rodeo, the long hard hours of hauling, for both her daughter's death and Nick's distance and had given up hoping he would walk away. When he wouldn't, she did.

A part of Malone had always believed Nick kept asking her out because he knew she would keep saying no. Another woman might make the mistake of saying yes and

Malone suspected Nick would have nothing to give.

Callahan grumbled, pulling her attention away from Nick momentarily.

"Malone, I've always wondered…"

At his hesitation, she looked back at him and waited.

"If it hadn't been me, if I hadn't been the one…" Nick's voice trailed away.

"To tell me about Tyge?" About the money he'd borrowed from Nick and others and couldn't pay. About the other women. She'd been living in denial. There'd been too many times he'd stayed gone a day longer than she'd expected, too many times he'd hit ignore on a phone call and not said why. She hadn't asked. She wouldn't be one of those women. If there wasn't trust, there was no reason for them to be together. No wedding bands, no certificate, no children.

For those reasons, and others, she'd trusted. For too long.

"Nick, I never blamed you. I'll always be grateful you were friend enough to tell me what I needed to hear."

The smile he gave her at the words was relieved but rueful. He placed his hat back on his head. "I'll be watching your run tonight, Malone. Good luck." He gave her a wink as he turned away. "And I *will* ask again."

She chuckled, feeling as if they'd passed some kind of relationship crisis. Nick was a decent man who deserved better than life had dealt him. She'd be sorry to lose his friendship over anything, much less over something she could neither change nor prevent.

* * *

Well, hmmm. It appears the gentleman would like to give Cade some competition in the romance department. Could I speak, I'd advise Cade to step up his game.

But human speech is not one of my skills and not—I can truthfully say—one I want, although it would make some of my discoveries much easier to disclose to those I try to help. Not that there's been much in the way of discoveries on who killed Walker. But I did find the spur. I'm convinced it's tied to the murder, and I did get it into Cade's hands. Even so, it has been remarkably hard to get to the heart of the matter. The goons who tried to pummel Tyge were hired by someone else. I'm sure of that. They weren't calling any shots, but someone somewhere is.

And I haven't found anything to tie that 'lost and found' spur to any person of interest. I've not seen a cowboy or cowgirl walking around with just one spur. It's always possible the murderer was a cowgirl. I've seen some with enough bulk and muscle to twist a man's neck with lethal force. Females aren't always the gentler of the species.

I decide to crawl through what seems a multitude of cattle trailers, most in need of a good scrubbing. I might come across some odor that's outside the expected. I'm no bloodhound, thank goodness, but I've encountered street drugs in our wanderings. It happens with life on the road. If marijuana or heroin or the nauseous smelling crystal meth were aboard any of these trailers, I'd know it.

I can't get to all of the trailers now, but it's a start. Unfortunately, the owners moved them from one point to another on the grounds for reasons I don't understand so it may be difficult to keep up with what I have and what I haven't inspected.

And I won't skip checking out the enclosed trailers. Some of them are pretty fancy and most are like Malone's and have living quarters which will be harder to access.

There's a lot left for me to do and not many clues to help me know where to look other than everywhere. After I make sure all is well with Malone and her foundling and let them know my need for food,

I'll continue the search.

As I turn to go, I hear sounds of an approach behind me, then voices, at which I move politely to one side of the wide corridor.

"What do you mean you're going to walk? Are you crazy?"

"Maybe, or maybe I'm coming to my senses."

Uh-oh, two arguing humans—and once again young males— are headed my way. With luck there'll be nothing more than a punch or two in the offing. I don't mind a good match as long as I'm an observer and not a participant.

I can defend myself better than most, hand-to-hand ... er paw- to-paw ... when I need to, but there's no reason to draw attention to myself without that need. That's a wise cat's first rule of business. Besides, I may already have made a name for myself with a few young outlaws coming to the Tyge's aid as I did. There was no help for it. A cat has to do what a cat has to do.

As they get closer, I can see they're of an age and a size and a swagger that brands them as rough stock competitors. Even the much older once-were's *and the very young* want-to-be's *have that same shoulders-back, loose-hipped walk.*

One strides ahead of the other, his cowboy hat shading his face, as if in a hurry. "I'm getting out, Dawson. If you're smart you will, too. This shit will get you killed."

The other grabs his shoulder and spins him around and I expect a blow to land.

"Damn it, Quinn, bailin' will get you killed faster. These bastards take care of business. Look what happened to Ro."

The two young men stand face-to-face, and I grasp they aren't at odds with each other despite the quarrelsome sound of their exchange. Their voices hold less anger than fear. Is this a piece of the puzzle or something unrelated?

"That wasn't about him getting out, that was about him getting greedy. I ain't greedy, and I didn't want in to start with. Hell, that first truck I drove wasn't supposed to have nothing but broncs. I didn't know until I made delivery what else I was carrying. I got suckered in."

"Yeah, but you took the payout and spent it. Kept your mouth shut just like I did."

"Wish to God I never had," *the one called Quinn turns and starts walking again.* "I'm going to finish the week 'cause my luck with the broncs is holding, then I'm disappearing back home for a year or two."

"You really think you can hide in them Louisiana swamps?"

"Damn right. I'll be with the snakes and the gators until I'm forgotten."

"You're kidding yourself!" *Quinn doesn't turn around at the rising level of the voice behind him.* "That bastard ain't ever going to forget your name or your face or the fact that you know too much."

The second cowboy waits in vain for a response then throws a costly-looking hat to the ground and kicks it. I sigh at the wastefulness of the young and almost miss his last rejoinder, spoken with a soft, rueful anger. "And he knows we're kin, you jackass."

A fact that will put the left-behind in some serious danger of retaliation, particularly if this outfit is being run like some kind of godfather gang.

Chapter 14

In spite of her mood, Malone smiled as she stepped into the trailer. Joss sat on the sleeper sofa with a handful of some of the brighter shirts from Malone's closet scattered around her. "I'm choosing for this performance," she pronounced, then asked, "Where've you been? Where's Callahan?"

As if on cue, a familiar bump at the door signaled the cat's return and Malone opened it wide enough for him to slide through. He leaped to the counter of the tiny kitchen area.

"Hungry, are you? Or thirsty?"

"He shouldn't be hungry. Luke brought him bacon and eggs for lunch."

Malone gave Joss a curious look.

A faint color tinged her cheeks. "I like him."

Malone heard the hint of defiance at the thought that she might object to his continued attentions. Malone tried to remember how she would have felt at that age, to imagine what Joss was feeling now. She couldn't. Beyond a doubt Joss was as headstrong, as strong willed as Malone had been. She wouldn't have survived if she hadn't been, at least not intact. But Joss had experienced things that had molded her in different ways than Malone's own life had done for her.

In the end, Malone nodded. "No reason not to. I've known the family for years. Brax and his wife did a good job raising him and his brothers."

"So … where've you been? Luke brought you something to eat, too."

Now it was Malone's turn to blush. The soft heat that hit her cheeks surprised her. Where had that come from?

"That was sweet of him, but Cade and I had some things to talk about so we grabbed a bite at a café just down the street."

Joss studied her face for a moment, then grinned. "I'm sure his parents did a good job of raising him, too."

Malone rolled her eyes but refused to take the bait, deciding simply to be glad that Joss had gained enough security in their roles to tease.

Joss's smile faded. "That Tyge came looking for you."

Malone studied her face. "What did he want?"

"I don't know. I was reading and had the door locked. I didn't open it, but I recognized his voice from the phone call."

If Malone could choose differently, she would not have listened to Tyge's message on the truck phone where Joss could overhear, but then neither would she have dreamed that he would get himself in what appeared to be a very perilous situation.

"Luke said somebody must have beat the sh … stew out of him. His face is pretty banged up."

All Malone could do was hope it had nothing to do with Roland Walker's death and be honest enough with Joss that she remained cautious. Not that Malone thought there was much chance she wouldn't. "You did well not to open the door. Tyge wouldn't hurt you. I'm sure of that. But I don't know what he's been into and who he's been running with the last few years. I'm guessing they aren't the nicest people in the world."

"He must have been a lot different when you were together."

"Well … yes and no … Tyge always had a bit of an edge to him, a wild side that tends to appeal to a teenage girl. I didn't give him a second look the first time I met him. He was a few years older, muscles all over from riding rough stock, so good-looking, but he was also a bit drunk and had a cute little redhead hanging all over him. He came after me, though. After that night."

"And you fell."

"Not at first. I made him work for it, but rodeo after rodeo he was there, helping me saddle, waiting for me after my run, cheering me on." She heard her own voice soften with memories. Cade had once done the same, but Cade had been away at college by then, chasing his own dreams. "We didn't travel far competing—Grandpa and me—just stuck with local runs. The small payouts looked big to me then. I found out later, Tyge let his buddies go on without him, following the big money, so he could chase after me."

"He loved you."

"He wanted me, for sure," Malone said drily.

"What did your grandpa think about him?"

"Not much. He never said so flat out, but Grandpa had a way of saying a lot in a very few words."

"You miss him."

"Always and forever. Grandpa and Grandma, both." And home. And she still had to decide about home.

"Well, looks like your grandpa was right." Joss gave her a quick look. "And you still need to stay away from Tyge."

"I plan on it. Now we need to get ready."

An hour later they stepped out of the living quarters with Callahan at their heels. "Why don't you go inside where it's warm?" Malone suggested.

"I'd rather come with you." Joss's tone was firm and Malone didn't argue. She was never sure if Joss was staying close for her own protection or Malone's.

"It's another hour before barrels. You aren't dressed very warm."

Joss ignored that. "Why do they stick to such set times … filling in with clown acts and local talent? It'd save a lot of time if they started one event right after another."

"Mostly for the fans. Some people care more about watching roping and maybe steer-wrestling. These are usually fans of the sport and not the thrill. There's a bigger crowd for rough stock riding. A lot of those are people you'd as easily find at monster truck jams and motocross. They like the excitement of knowing that someone could get hurt."

"Sounds sick to me."

Malone laughed. "Not necessarily. It isn't that they *want* someone to get hurt. Some wish they had the courage or freedom to risk themselves for a sport they love. It takes them out of what can seem to be a dull world."

"Do the sponsors follow the fans more than they do the competitors?"

"For the most part. Sponsors as well as the vendors who pay a hefty fee to set up at these events, but it brings in the sales, now and later."

"Sure are a lot of them. You can buy anything and everything without ever leaving the place. From hats and boots to jeans and jewelry."

"You see something you like?" Malone asked.

"Every time I turn around," Joss admitted, "but nothing I need."

Malone made a mental note to find a reason for a shopping trip the next day.

"I thought I'd walk a few blocks south of here in the morning. I used your cell phone to look up a cute little salon that specializes in short cuts. I made an appointment." She hesitated. "I guess I should have asked first."

"Of course, you can use it. But … are you sure? Your hair is gorgeous and you've already cut so much of it."

"I like it a lot better short. It's easier and … cute. I haven't been allowed to cut it for a while. And I, for sure, need someone to straighten out the mess I made of it."

The implications of that saddened Malone while Joss's wanting to look cute—for Luke?—heartened her. "Will you give up wearing a cap all the time?"

Joss gave her an *almost* smile. "Most of the time, anyway."

"Did you happen to notice if they did nails?"

"I think so."

"Good, I'll try to get an appointment close to yours

and then we'll have some lunch away from here."

"Lots of choices right here on the grounds," Joss said.

"And none of them really healthy, now, are they?"

Joss hesitated. "I'll need some money."

"You know where your money is. I've put it away every day."

"I haven't earned it yet. I'm still paying off the clothes you bought me—I kept every tag so I'd know—and I know how much I eat."

Malone shot her a look. "The money is yours." She left it at that.

They reached the barn and Jaz's stall and Malone started laughing. "*That* is why you've earned your pay. I *hate* braiding manes." The mane wasn't simply braided, it was woven into a fancy lattice-work of hair. Malone did the bare minimum necessary to keep from grabbing flowing mane rather than reins in her run, but she had to admit the animal looked *photo ready*. And she always bought one of the professional photographs of herself during a performance, most at the first or second barrel going into or coming out of the tight turns although she had a few where she and her horse were breezing for home, hair, mane, and tail flying.

"Hey, beautiful." Malone turned, startled at Cade's voice behind her. Before she could speak, he waved his hand negligibly in her direction. "Not you. This gorgeous creature."

Stepping forward, he ran a hand over the mare's gleaming shoulder.

And Malone laughed again. Glad that she could, with all the drama that had happened in the past few days, with all that had—and hadn't—happened between the two of them over the past many years.

* * *

I'm a creature of instinct rather than habit, and instinct tells me that my plan to stick close to Joss this evening may not be needed.

With a slight signal, Cade attaches Townie to Joss's heel as we all part ways. That Aussie, like most dogs, is bound by habit as I am not, but more, is bound by obedience as I most surely am not. With Cade accompanying Malone and Townie guarding Joss, I am free to surveil the premises. The only bad part is that, once again, I'm forced to admit the dog has his uses.

I start in outlying areas, looking for anything that is out of place, then drift closer to the action in the arena when all seems quiet on the perimeter. I hear the announcer declare the end of the steer wrestling—a silly event with the cowboy leaping from a speeding horse to grab a steer by the horns and force him to the ground—with bronc riding being next up. Having become familiar with the line-up of events, I know that barrel racing will follow bronc riding, both saddle bronc and bareback. I don't want to miss Malone's performance.

My next area of surveillance will be behind the bucking chutes. Rough stock riding isn't my favorite rodeo event. I can't understand the incredible stupidity that causes a human to climb aboard a massive package of muscle determined to unseat him and then stomp him into the ground if at all possible.

With that said, I've noted rough-stock contestants tend to leave their duffle bags lying open in a trusting, if careless, manner. I don't know what, if anything, I could find, but you never know until you look. Most of them are as studious to their craft as are ropers and bulldoggers and barrel racers but, beyond a doubt, their ranks have been infiltrated by not just the undesirable but the unlawful—and maybe even the deadly. The last quarrel I overhead made that more than clear. As I make my way from one end of the coliseum to the other, the clowns assume position on the arena floor for a brief comedic act while the rodeo announcer proclaims the gate will soon be opening on the first bronc rider of the evening. I listen as he begins his spiel about bronc riding being the more potentially dangerous of the rough stock events despite the hazards of a bull's horns.

I watch those broncs trot down an alleyway that runs parallel to the corridor where I stand. Almost within touching distance, if I were that dumb. With a little cowboy encouragement of yipping and yaying—which sounds are not just on Dax's phone screen, after all—they make their way into a series of holding pens where gates are closed behind them. I peer into eyes that, while watchful, don't seem the least wild and rank. In fact, most appear to hold a spark of interest in their new surroundings. However, the man on the loudspeaker assures his audience that many broncs tend to turn dangerous hooves upon a rider once he's thrown, making me wonder if that was perhaps the forbearer to the phrase kick a man while he's down.

His patter helps the antics of the clowns fill the void, although I suspect diehard fans of rough stock riding are more inclined to use the facilities and buy another alcoholic beverage than they are to get bored and leave.

I relegate his voice to background noise and don't doubt many spectators do the same. My attention is fixed on greater things though I'll stay in tune enough that I don't miss the end of bronc riding and the start of barrel racing that will follow.

Despite my own expectations on the subject, I've found barrel racing to be a sport I can like. The riders are dedicated and skilled, their horses athletic and talented. The bursts of speed and fast turns combine for a breathtaking performance that thrills the crowd.

I pick a spot to perch and allow myself to watch the bare bronc riding, to be sure I don't miss Malone's performance in the next event.

As the gate is flung open for each bronc, the whooping and hollering of the cowboys around me is deafening, but I feel heartened that they appear to be cheering each other on rather than hoping for defeat of what must—many times—be a competitor who stands between them and a paycheck. I suspect it's the same with the bull riders.

In fact, each competitor seems to have a posse—that's what they call themselves and it's nothing to do with law and order—of two or three fellow competitors. These trusted mates help him settle upon the broad back of his ride and ensure his rigging is secure before the tip of his hat signals the opening of the gate. Once the animal makes his explosive escape from the narrow chute into the arena, they continue their support with shouts of encouragement, which the rider can't possibly hear over the blare of the speaker and the snorts of his draw.

I don't have long to wait before bronc riding concludes and there's another intermission. At last, Malone enters the arena on the powerfully built horse called Jaz, which name probably makes perfect sense to someone somewhere. She covers the ground as effortlessly as a train steams along its track, heeding signals that are invisible to the uneducated among the spectators. But I've watched Malone as she does what she calls 'tuning'. Her slow work in the practice pen mimics the moves she makes at incredible speeds during a performance. And the signals vary from horse to horse. A stride or two from the barrel, she sits in preparation for the turn. One horse will require nothing more to slow than that fraction required. One will need a softly voiced 'whoa'. Yet another will require a soft 'bump' of the reins. It's a fascinating art. Absolutely fascinating. And the horses—at least the ones Malone rides—all enjoy their jobs. That's evident in their eagerness to enter the arena.

I experience a strong feeling of pride as she exits the arena after a flawless performance. She is, after all, my human for the present. I hear the announcer declare hers as the time to beat so far tonight but cautions there are yet more outstanding horses and riders to come. That may be true, but they'll have to work hard for their money.

Now for the task at hand.

There may be those who find the bawling of cattle a familiar, even welcome, sound. For me, it's an unharmonious din, though the bulls themselves don't seem to realize the fact.

And the contestants don't seem to mind it, but that could be because the clatter they make combined with the noise of the loudspeaker is equal in decibels. I skirt those contestants, keeping to the periphery of careless boots. Fortunately, most in this vicinity cling to fence railings or climb up to sit in precarious positions for a better visual of what's happening in the arena.

I'm careful to keep my movements discreet and hesitate at the sight of Tyge with his back propped against a corner post. He seems more interested in studying the faces around him than in the arena action and—as Luke described to Joss—his own is badly 'banged up'. His gaze skims over me without recognition. I shouldn't be surprised. Past behavior has made it clear that a cat, regardless of my actions to save his skin, is beneath his notice. He sits unusually quiet and still, almost as if he's hiding in plain sight. I keep my attention half with him as I make my way from duffle to duffle. I'm clever at appearing bored and feel sure none of the humans is going to notice my search. The first few bags hold only ropes and gloves and containers of rosin, a substance the cowboys use on their ropes.

Something dark and metallic catches my eye in one, and I circle from a different angle to catch a better look. The short barrel of a handgun gives me pause, but I accept there's nothing to be done about it. By the time I find Cade and convince him to follow, the duffle and its owner could be long gone, and I'll have missed any opportunity to determine the owner's identity.

As if to prove that probability, the announcer strikes up once again while the first of the bulls are moved into the bucking chutes. 'Ladies and gentlemen, like the broncs, these bulls are more powerful and muscular than even a decade ago.

They are the result of selective breeding. Their physical attributes have been pulled to the fore by genetics. Watch as their hoofs hit the ground with incredible force, jump to extraordinary heights and twist and turn midair with amazing agility."

After a moment, I tune him out. I resume my search of cowboy gear but see nothing more that appears to be a possible problem. I'm careful to note which cowboy retrieves the bag with the handgun, but I don't recognize him. I will in the future and not just because of my photographic memory. The scar low on one jaw, though barely visible in the dim light, is distinct in appearance, almost a tiny starburst. If that saw a surgeon's hand, it was an unskilled one.

With my focus still partly on Tyge, I'm aware when he shifts positions as the cowboy in question passes him by. Shifts and stares but makes no other move. Unlike myself, the cowboy never even notices. Humans are so incredibly unobservant.

Tyge watches as the space around us empties then refills with bull riders. I make note of the fact that the exchange isn't complete. Some contestants trade the number previously affixed to their shirts for a different one, close one duffle and open another. The implications are obvious and amazing. It must take a special kind of stupid to want to ride both bulls and broncs.

Despite my careful exploration, other than the handgun, which isn't all that uncommon these days, I see nothing more among the collection of cowboy gear that I think noteworthy. I guess I've found all that I can here, and it's little enough. Too little.

I cast one last glance toward the chutes before going in search of food. But I stop when I hear that the first cowboy to ride will be Quinn, and his lead posse member appears to be the kin whose argument I overheard earlier. I swiftly alter course, hoping to gather at least one tidbit of information from tonight's work. I listen to their banter. Whatever rancor was between them seems to have dissipated, but that's the way of humans, unpredictable in their emotions. For now, they appear to have resolved their difference of opinion as kith and kin often do. I hear the excitement in Quinn's voice as he climbs up the chute and peers down at the bull.

"Dawson." Catching the cowboy's attention, Quinn hands his bull rope to the other and climbs over to settle on the broad, muscular back of his ride.

I almost miss the exchange. It's because I'm watching Dawson's face and note the faint, but distinct, look of regret that I catch the surreptitious movement that follows. Quinn's bull rope is dropped to the ground and Dawson pulls a substitute from a bag lying at his feet. A feeling of dread sweeps me, and I yowl a warning that my intellect tells me Quinn cannot hear above the clamor around him and would not understand if he did hear. This cannot end well for Quinn.

I leap forward, but know I'm already too late as the gate is swung wide. I hear shouts of dismay and a thud. The bull is spinning free and riderless in the arena. Quinn is crumpled on the ground half in, half out of the chute. I can't tell if he lives and can't help him regardless. I focus my attention on Dawson who is crouched beside him and—had I not witnessed the exchange of the bull rope—I could believe the anguish on his face to be genuine. And Dawson's guilt, too, I can do nothing about. At least for the moment.

What I can do is find the evidence of the crime, for I've no doubt a crime of monumental proportion has been committed. Then I see it. The switched bull rope lies in the dirt of the chute near Dawson. His shoulder is to it as well as to me as he focuses on Quinn. One slight shift and he'll see me and the rope.

I snag and drag the rope under the chute. I give a quick look around, but no one is watching. I'm confident no one notices as I bury it close to a corner post as deeply as speed allows. Fortunately, there's a mix of shavings and sawdust everywhere. It's as safe as I can make it until I can bring it to the attention of Cade.

Chapter 15

Cade moved quickly in and out of the crowd as the ambulance, lights flashing but siren off as requested, pulled as close to the back of the chutes as possible. The announcer was assuring the crowd that emergency assistance was at hand as both ambulance and driver were paid to be at each and every performance throughout the event. If everyone would please keep their seat, the cowboy would receive the best possible care.

But Cade had seen Quinn Riverstock hit the chute with a force equivalent to a passenger without a seatbelt ejected from a car in a crash. If the bull rider lived long enough to get that care it would be a minor miracle.

Since he'd been at the far side of the arena, he reached the bucking chutes as a stretcher was being placed on the ground beside Riverstock. The bull rider's twisted torso brought a sick feeling to Cade's stomach. This wasn't a case of a cowboy concussed and momentarily unconscious. Riverstock could not have gotten to his feet regardless.

Cade's gaze swept the scene and found nothing to explain what had happened. Riverstock's glove was still fastened to his hand so the force of the bull's leap, twist, and turn hadn't caused it to tear lose. Cade suspected, if he checked, he'd find rosin had been carefully applied, providing just that much more grip. Riverstock wasn't some yahoo rough stock rider. He was a year-end finalist in a multimillion-dollar association. He knew his job.

The EMTs stabilized then maneuvered the cowboy onto the stretcher with as much finesse as was possible given the circumstances. Cade tried to read their expressions, but they were professionals, and their faces gave nothing away of their assessment of his condition. One spoke into a small headset before they lifted the stretcher and began easing their way back to the ambulance.

Cade was pleased to see his staff keeping the milling cowboys shepherded back and out of the way. Only one competitor hovered beside the stretcher, then one of the flank men placed a hand on the cowboy's shoulder gently urged him aside. When he turned to stare at the stretcher as it was carried away, Cade recognized him. Dawson White was another bull rider, one he'd seen frequently in Riverstock's company. It would be unimaginably hard to see a friend in that kind of shape. Harder yet to climb on a bull's back moments later and complete a successful ride. But that's what these competitors would be required to do moments from now, knowing that Riverstock was being sped to the hospital, not knowing his fate. Cade made a mental note to speak with Dawson before his ride.

Even as the lights of the ambulance disappeared from sight, the announcer was sweeping the crowd back to the performance, reminding them that every cowboy who'd ridden a bronc earlier or would step down onto a bull in this event put himself—life and limb—at risk.

Cade moved into the crowd of cowboys and made a split-second decision to do something he'd never before had occasion to do and hoped he never did again. Signaling them to move away from the chutes and the blare of the loudspeaker, he waited until they quieted and focused their attention on him.

"What just happened was rough. Bad. I know you're all rattled. What I want to know is whether you want to move forward with this event tonight or if you want to push it out." The crowd would be disappointed and some sponsors might complain, but his primary concern was the safety of the contestants. If they couldn't focus, the risks of them climbing on a bull became exponentially greater.

After some shuffling of feet and whispers amongst themselves, one said quietly, "We'll ride."

Cade took a moment to search their faces, then nodded. He understood and respected that decision. He looked for Dawson among those gathered and didn't see him. For a moment, he wondered if Quinn's friend had followed the ambulance. Then he saw him close to the bucking chute that had been the scene of the accident.

He walked over as the cowboy kicked at the dust in the chute. As Cade neared, one of the staff called. "Here it is, Dawson. I've got it."

Dawson reached for the bull rope as the staffer handed it to him.

"That Quinn's?" Cade asked.

"Yeah. He'll want it." Dawson studied the rig in his hands, a faint frown upon his face. He glanced at Cade then turned away abruptly. "I'll put it in his bag and get it to him at the hospital when I'm done here."

"You going to be okay to ride?" Cade knew Dawson hadn't heard the question he'd put to the others, suspected he'd be the most shaken among them.

"Sure. Yeah. Sure."

And even though Cade himself wasn't sure how *okay* the cowboy would be, the choice was his to make. He watched as Dawson walked away with Quinn's bull rope, twisting and turning the rig in his hand as he looked down at it. Probably wondering what the hell had gone so wrong in that chute when the gate swung open, Cade thought, just like they all were.

Cade said a quiet prayer as he propped himself against a post. He'd watch from here until this event was over. He'd seen all kinds of wrecks through his rodeo years, seen competitors injured, even killed, and most had been due to some freakish but explainable incident. He had no explanation for what had happened to Quinn. He hoped the cowboy survived, and, if he did, maybe he could provide an answer of some kind.

The second cowboy out of the chute completed his ride without incident, but Cade suspected he'd be disappointed with the less than stellar performance that was reflected in his score. No doubt his head wasn't in the game and with good reason. As the gate opened on the next ride, Cade heard Callahan's yowl in almost the same moment he felt a firm tug on the knee of his jeans.

He glanced down at the gray cat and had a moment's

confusion. The cat sat amid a tangled length of thickly braided rope. Recognition dawned as he caught sight of the cowbell, whose weight allowed the rope to fall off the bull when a cowboy's ride was over, attached. The rope was a bull rope and the rosin that had been applied had picked up a significant amount of sawdust and shavings, probably as Callahan had dragged it over to him.

When he bent to pick it up, Callahan sat back on his haunches with a satisfied air. Cade could almost see the word *finally* as a cartoon bubble over the cat's head. But he suspected this particular bull rope signified something far less funny than a cartoon. That suspicion was so strong he was almost hesitant to put his hand on it. Callahan's vigilant stare didn't allow for that as an option.

In the same heartbeat of time that he straightened, rope in hand, he saw it. The handle, braided into the center, had been severed nearly in half at one end. The smooth edges of the cut sides told a clear story. The edges on the other side were frayed where they'd given way to the g-force of the bull's bulk twisting and turning in the air. It had been carefully thought through, skillfully done by someone who knew the sport intimately, who knew and was known by the rider. Onlookers would have been unable to see the damage and unlikely to notice even had it been obvious. The cowboy, himself, would have checked his gear earlier, handed his rig to someone he trusted to have his back so he could focus his attention on the bull whose number he'd drawn.

Cade wished he were wrong, wished like hell he wasn't seeing what was before his eyes.

He met Callahan's steady gaze and gave the cat a nod. What the hell. One or both of them was a loony tune.

Or maybe it was neither. On that possibility, he pulled his phone from his pocket and made the call to Ryder.

Ending the call, he looked up and saw Tyge watching him from a distance away.

* * *

At the end of the night's performance, Cade waited patiently while competitors and staff assembled around him on the arena floor. The space was remarkably quiet with the announcer on the floor with them. Even the din of the ever-present animals was muted in the background.

Aleta, who'd put the word out for him that everyone was to gather for a brief meeting, stood close to his side, clipboard in hand, alert and prepared as always. His gaze sought and found Malone, and he realized she centered him in a way no one ever had. She was the missing piece of his life. He put that thought aside to address the crowd waiting for him to speak.

Though he didn't turn on the mike he held in one hand, his voice carried clearly, even echoing faintly. "Thank you for coming. I won't keep you long. One of our own was hurt tonight, and each and every one of you handled yourself and the unfortunate accident professionally and respectfully. I want you to know how much I appreciate that fact, how much I appreciate each one of you."

Cade hesitated. Even now, as he was calling it an accident, he was convinced that Callahan was right. It was not a mishap that had sent Riverstock on an ambulance speeding through the city.

"I know you're waiting to hear how Quinn is doing. All I can tell you is he's in surgery. I'm headed to the hospital when we finish here, and I'll share what I can as soon as I can. Over the next few days, Aleta will have updates in the show office as we get them." If the cowboy lived that long. The thought lingered in his mind, but those were words he wouldn't say.

Stepping back, he handed the microphone to a steer wrestler who also frequently held Cowboy Church services when on the road. The man led them in prayer and asked them to continue praying for their fellow competitor and his family in the days to come.

Aleta waited with him while the staff and contestants dispersed. "What else, boss?"

"I won't know more until I get to the hospital."

"Wait," she put a hand on his arm as he turned away. "That veterinary intern you want me to keep busy? She's not worth crap for office work. What am I supposed to do with her?"

In as few words as possible, he explained Deputy Armand's true identity and reason for her presence, watching as her eyes widened. He ended with, "Bottom line, I suspect she needs an excuse to get out and about the grounds. So, without letting her know you know, explain some of the staff functions and tell her you'd like for her to be productive while she's here and not just another pretty face." He paused. "If she is? Pretty that is." The comment could be unfortunate if she were not.

Aleta nodded. "Very."

"Anyway, ask her what she can do to lighten the load you have and then allow her whatever latitude she takes."

"And I'm supposed to explain that to the rest of the staff, how?"

Cade shrugged and answered even as his gaze and

thoughts tracked Malone across the arena. He wanted her to go to the hospital with him. "However you can. That's why you're my right hand and lead staff member and why you're the only one of them who's going to know who and what she is."

Aleta rolled her eyes and started away from him but decided to have the last word. "You'd better hustle, Malone is getting away."

Cade stifled both a retort and a curse word as he saw Malone exit with Joss at the far end of the arena.

Aleta's soft laugh, still holding a tinge of sadness from the night's disastrous ride, drifted over her shoulder.

* * *

Cade's long, focused stride reached Malone's trailer almost before she and Joss did. Townsend had been forced to trot to keep up. Malone turned with a look of surprise as he called her name.

"Go to the hospital with me?"

Joss raised her brows, and Cade gave her what was intended to be a quelling look. She proved it totally ineffective when she lifted one brow, crossed her arms, and leaned against the side of the trailer.

Malone nodded. "I can do that. Let me grab a jacket."

As she stepped inside, Cade turned his attention to Joss who continued wearing that almost-grin. "I'm leaving Townsend with you and Callahan. Keep the door locked until we get back, okay?"

"Sure." Joss let go of the smile as a hint of worry crept into her eyes. "But don't keep Malone out too much later. She's tired."

"I won't."

Townsend gave a soft woof as the gray cat strolled into view and sat at Joss's boots. The cat gave Cade a look as if to say *I've got this*. And perhaps—just perhaps—Cade thought, he did.

When Malone stepped back out, she wore a crimson jacket with a soft black fur collar that appealed to him on every level, even the fact that—knowing Malone—he more than suspected the fur of being imitation. The vivid color, the woman, the brush of fur against her smooth neck drew a visceral response.

Giving Cade a final look of warning, Joss stepped inside with Callahan. Once they heard the sound of the deadbolt sliding home behind Joss and her companions for the night, Malone and Cade were on their way.

With a click of his remote, Cade started his truck from half a parking lot away. It wouldn't make it entirely warm when they got there, but it did help remove a bit of the chill before he opened the door on the passenger side for Malone.

She had her seatbelt secure before he slid in on the driver's side. He felt her watching him as he pulled up the address of the hospital on the truck's navigation screen. "What's going on, Cade?"

"Show that much, huh?"

"Maybe not to everyone."

It surprised him a little that she'd admit it and pleased him even more. "I'm not sure Quinn Riverstock's accident was accidental." He told her about the rope that Callahan had brought to his attention. "It sounds crazy, I know."

"I'm sure it would to the authorities," she said dryly, then added more slowly, "but there's something about that cat."

"Yeah," he agreed, "but not something easily explained.

Ryder's going to think I'm a nut case."

"You called him?"

"He's meeting us at the hospital." Cade had second-guessed himself ever since he'd made the call, but he didn't know what the hell else to do. Lives were at stake.

When they walked into the crowded waiting room, Ryder wasn't the only lawman present. Detective Marchmann stood propped against a wall near the entrance, glowering. He straightened as soon as he caught sight of Cade. His scowl deepened.

Ignoring Marchmann, Cade moved Malone past him, toward the huddle of Quinn's friends and fellow competitors. Some lifted red-rimmed eyes to nod at him, others sat with heads down as Cade touched a back or a shoulder. They didn't know and didn't care who offered comfort. A few stood as still as sentinels, their backs to the wall, staring outward with thoughts focused inward.

Cade could almost read those thoughts. Life was short. Life was sweet. Sure, they took risks. Every day. It was what they loved, how they earned a living, some of them with families to feed. They knew the penalty for failure, but still … it wasn't supposed to be like this. This was never really supposed to happen.

There was one girl among them but not part of them. She twisted and retwisted the straps of her purse, staring down at her high-heeled boots. Cade couldn't see her face, just the fall of gilt hair that hid her features from sight. He would have comforted her but was too wise to believe that he could. He sighed and turned to face the business at hand, callous as that seemed. But he had one murder on his hands, already, and he couldn't be sure Quinn wasn't an attempted murder. If he was, Cade hope liked hell the 'attempted' aspect stood firm.

Marchmann stood in the center of the wide exit to the hallway as if he suspected Cade might flee. Cade sent a questioning look toward Ryder who shrugged and grimaced. It was clear he wasn't enjoying the detective's presence. That didn't enlighten Cade as to who had alerted the local authorities to the injury, but it did clarify that it hadn't been the U.S. Marshal.

With a last glance at the cowboys scattered around waiting for news on Quinn, hoping against hope, Cade motioned to the lawmen to follow him out into the hall. He kept a protective arm around Malone, drawing her with him when she might have lingered in the waiting area.

The detective was first to speak but he, at least, kept his voice low. "You want to explain why a federal marshal is here?"

Taking a chance—one he considered a fairly safe bet—Cade said with equal quiet and much less belligerence, "Have you tried asking him?"

"Said he got a tip." Marchmann's irritation was blatant.

"I can speak for myself," Ryder said with a grunt. "I get lots of tips. Some pan out, some don't. If I start giving away my sources, I won't have to worry with wasting time on the ones that don't. Then again, I won't have the benefit of the ones that do either."

"Did your source happen to link the cowboy in surgery with a broken back to the one in the morgue with a broken neck?" Marchmann's tone was as blunt as his words.

Cade felt as much as heard Malone's sudden intake of breath. He sent the detective a heated glare.

The detective glared right back. "What? You don't even think this was suspicious, Delaney? I'm telling you now, you got anything says this wasn't an accident, you'd better lay it out. I've already heard the whisperings in that room. His friends aren't buying that it was an accident. Said Riverstock was as good as they come and had his butt tight as a tick on that bull." He nodded what passed for an apology at Malone. "Their words not mine."

He waited a moment and, when Cade didn't answer, snapped his fingers as he threatened, "I'm that close to arresting your ass."

"For what?"

"Obstruction of justice."

Abruptly, Cade decided it might be time to take himself out of the middle. He trusted Ryder to find answers more than he did Marchmann, but the association couldn't afford the bad press of their operations director being arrested. It might only be for the briefest span of time, so Marchmann could have his moment of revenge, but it could have lasting impact on the association. As long as Ryder heard the information at the same time as Marchmann, the federal agent could get his hands on it through other means.

"Well," Marchmann pressed, "do you have evidence of foul play?"

"I have a bull rope that appears to be tampered with, but I've no idea whether or not it was Quinn's." That was a flat-out lie. He had a very good idea that it was. Just no proof.

"And it was at the scene of the crime?" Marchmann almost pounced on Cade's admission.

"I don't know that there was a crime." Cade gave that a moment to sink in then asked, "Do you?"

"If there was, I'll find out. And I don't need help from the feds or obstacles from you. Was it close to the fallen cowboy?" He didn't even pretend patience with the question.

"Not when it was brought to my attention." Cade wished he could enjoy baiting the pompous idiot, but the reality of Quinn's injuries was too close, too raw.

"Brought to your attention? By who?" Marchmann clearly didn't enjoy pulling information from Cade.

"By Callahan."

"Callahan?" the detective almost sneered. "Is that some cowboy nickname?"

"No nickname and no cowboy. Callahan is a cat, a gray cat who travels with Ms. Summers here."

Cade chanced a glance her way. She was looking at the local officer with her chin tilted and her brow lifted, daring, just daring him, to say anything derogatory. Even so, Cade caught the look she cast his way. She was no doubt thinking he was crazy and maybe he was. The expression on the detective's face spoke volumes.

"Damn it, Delaney. I want to know who the hell brought you that rope."

"I told you. The cat brought it to me."

"You have a rope that wasn't by the chute where Quinn Riverstock was hurt. That may or may not be his. And it was brought to you by a cat."

With feet planted, Marchmann had leaned closer toward him with each word, so much so Cade thought he might topple over.

"I don't know where it was when Callahan found it." Tired of the game, Cade kept his voice quiet but taunting. "It may or may not have been by the chute. It may or may not be Quinn's. But it was brought to me by the cat."

Ryder actually chuckled, and Cade didn't trust himself

to look that way and keep a straight face, but Marchmann shot him an evil look before turning his attention back to Cade. "Where is this rope now?"

"It's in my truck. Since I can't say for sure it has any significance with what happened to Quinn, I didn't want to drag it in here. No way to know how long it had been buried in the dirt." He lifted a brow, questioning Marchmann's next move.

"I'll walk out with you and take a look at it, but Delaney, you'd better figure out what kind of outfit you're running here—or I'll figure it out for you."

"I've got nothing better to do," Ryder inserted smoothly. "I may as well join y'all."

Cade looked at Malone, and she shook her head. "That girl in the waiting room … I think she's Quinn's fiancée. I'll go sit with her awhile."

He touched her cheek softly, mentally daring Marchmann to say an impatient word at the delay. "I won't be long."

Chapter 16

Unfortunately, Cade was gone five minutes too long. When he returned, Malone looked at him numbly over the shoulder of the weeping young woman, hearing but not really absorbing the curses of Quinn Riverstock's friends. The doctor had been brief, but compassionate, though his face had revealed what he thought of a sport that had taken a young man's life.

Cade's face was just as reflective. Malone knew the moment he realized the shift in the waiting room from fear and hope to grief and fury. The only thing she saw in the silver gaze that never left her face as he crossed to her side was sorrowful regret at the ending of a life.

She released Quinn's fiancée to the arms of a trio of girlfriends who had entered on Cade's heels, shock etched on their faces as they realized the worst for Quinn had transpired. Although Malone never truly believed that death *was* the worst that could happen to a person. There were things she would not want to survive.

Thoughts tumbled through her mind as Cade pulled her in close to his chest and pressed his lips to her forehead. "Let's go home."

For a moment, she wondered, truly wondered, what it would be like if she could do just that. Go home—with Cade—to a home that they shared, the home she'd once dreamed about. She shook off the thought as they walked through the silent halls of the hospital. She had other dreams now. Bigger dreams, but, perhaps, not sweeter ones.

* * *

Townie bumps into me yet again with his restless pacing and I swat him, though I'm careful to keep my claws sheathed. He's a nuisance, but I understand his agitation. There's something about the atmosphere beyond this cozy abode that is unsettled. At this time of night, the area is normally filled with voices and laughter as contestants return to trailers and settle in. Now the doors of vehicles and living quarters slam shut and echo across the asphalt, unaccompanied by human voice. A dog barks once and is quickly hushed by some unheard someone. Townsend lifts his head and pricks his ears at the sound then subsides without his usual low response.

Death does that, and this one has affected many. I'm as confident that Quinn has died as I am that he was murdered by his own kin. Hopefully the clue of the bull rope I was able to seize and deliver to Cade will help with a conviction. My next mission is to identify him to Cade. Though I'm confident it won't be an easy task, I know I'll find a way.

I watch as Joss lies down on the sleeper couch and Townsend seeks permission to join her with a steady stare. She pats the coverlet, and he leaps lightly up to settle beside her. I take a vigilant position beside the front door, ready to attack and defend should the occasion arise. I don't anticipate that it will and certainly hope that it won't. I'm not a warrior, but can, and will, hold my own in a scuffle if it's brought to me.

Despite Joss's reclining pose, I sense her tension. She looks my way from time to time, and I try to look as nonchalant as I can, but she's not reassured by the fact that I begin my nightly grooming. Joss isn't fooled by my air of indifference, proving herself, as the old adage goes, wise beyond her years.

At a rap on the door, her indrawn breath is sharp and deep. Her eyes widen as she stares at the knob. I know terror when I see it. Townsend growls deep in his throat, but she places her hand lightly on his head, and he does not bark. Good dog.

"Malone?"

Tyge's voice. Fear gone, Joss rolls her eyes. But she makes no move to open the door, and she doesn't answer even when he calls out again for Malone.

His boot heels strike hard on the pavement as he stalks away. In the silence that follows, I ponder his persistence in wanting to speak with Malone. I don't sense that he means harm to her. But it could have been triggered by his enemies. He seems to have plenty of those. Does he fear they might think Malone has some knowledge of their wrongdoings through her association with him? And are his enemies and Quinn Riverstock's the same? If I were a betting cat, I'd place money on a yes there.

Little time passes after Tyge's visit before a key turns in the lock. As Malone steps in, I slip out. I'm restless with the sense that events are escalating and that danger encircles Tyge. Saving him from himself could be a byproduct of my efforts, but my focus is on protecting Malone and Joss from becoming collateral damage.

* * *

Malone stared down at the hand she had stretched in front of the manicurist, then closed her eyes. Although she'd lost her enthusiasm for the bit of pampering, she and Joss had still made the trip to the salon. She'd been pleased when the tiny, rather plain entry opened into a very upscale space filled with light and elegance. Joss was swept away by an enthusiastic woman with flaming red hair and a smattering of freckles across her nose and cheeks. Malone's manicurist was male with a shaved head and kind, brown eyes.

"You seem tense," he said as he studied her hands, which she knew were pretty much a mess. Today's manicure would quickly become a casualty of her way of life. "Would you like a glass of wine?"

That surprised a chuckle from her. "It's ten in the morning."

He smiled broadly. "A Bloody Mary, then? We'll call it brunch."

She hesitated, tempted more than she would have thought. Any alcohol in the drink would be long gone before her run tonight. But she had a full afternoon in front of her, so she shook her head.

When asked to select a color for her nails, she leaned back in the very comfortable chair and closed her eyes. "Surprise me."

"Ah, I was right." She heard a hint of an accent in his voice but didn't try to place it. "You have a trusting soul and a brave one."

Malone returned the smile she heard in his voice but didn't open her eyes. She'd trusted too much for too many years. She really suspected she didn't have a lot of trust left in her. As for courage … she'd never stopped to consider or question whether or not she was brave. Maybe that teenage girl had been, or maybe she'd just been headstrong and foolish. In the years since, Malone had simply put one foot in front of the other, digging in, building the life she wanted, creating the security she needed. The color of her nails wasn't a matter of daring. How she appeared to others was of far less consequence than how she felt about herself.

She'd begun to get that feeling about Joss, as well. There were insecurities about the girl, but they weren't emotional ones. Joss had a strong sense of self.

Nevertheless, when her nails were dry, and Joss walked out of the back of the salon, Malone knew her jaw dropped. The natural blonde hair that had slowly begun to emerge from cheap dark dye with each day's shower now shimmered with highlights, and there was no longer any evidence of the chopped look Joss had created with a pair of barn shears. Clearly, the stylist who had taken her in hand was as much an artist as Malone's manicurist had proven to be. The short locks were feathered enchantingly around her face. Joss wasn't simply a pretty, young girl. She had truly beautiful features that would carry gracefully into maturity and beyond.

When Malone said as much, Joss smiled although her eyes still reflected sadness from the events of the previous night. "I sure don't look like the old me."

And Malone knew that was what mattered most to the girl. That she not be recognized. Still, Malone could see a hint of shyness in Joss's smile as she added, "I think Luke will like it. Now let me see your nails."

As Malone obliged, holding them up and wiggling them lightly in the air, Joss said softly, "Oh, how pretty. You let him do tiny stars! And a moon. And little crosses. Look at the detail!"

"Well, my eyes were closed, and he didn't ask so I didn't have to answer." Malone studied her nails, silently pleased. The man had proven himself an artist and she'd tipped that artistry generously, as she would Joss's stylist. Her nails were a shimmery cream and the stars and moon and crosses were all a pale gold. "It will be a real shame to be scrubbing water buckets with these hands this afternoon."

Moments later, they took to the sidewalk and strolled past several ethnic restaurants that would have seriously tempted Malone if they were having dinner, but with all she had to do each afternoon she was looking for lighter fare and allowed Joss to pull her into a small café where they ordered soup and salad.

Joss seized one of the rolls they were brought with their glasses of ice water and, after slathering it from a crockery bowl of whipped butter, ate it with the appetite of the young and always-famished. The meal that followed was delicious, and they chatted about the horses while they ate. Malone sometimes thought Joss had more questions than any teenager she'd ever been around.

When Joss's plate and bowl were empty, she picked up the last bread roll and offered it to Malone. When Malone smiled and shook her head, Joss buttered it, her motions slowing. Malone noted a faint frown creasing her forehead. She didn't say anything about it, but wasn't surprised when Joss lifted unexpectedly troubled eyes to her.

"I've been thinking."

Malone waited silently.

"There's something I need to do, but I'm afraid."

"Tell me."

"First, you need to know a couple of things. When you asked if I'd broken any laws…?"

Malone nodded, still silent but now concerned as well.

"I said I hadn't, and I don't think I did. If you hurt someone in self-defense that's not a crime, is it?"

"Probably not but it depends on the circumstances. Before we get into that what is the second thing?"

"Someone could come looking for me."

"I gathered that much on my own. Otherwise, you wouldn't have been trying to disguise your looks. Family?" She'd asked that question once, but Joss had said there were none.

"No."

"Then the *someone* you hurt in self-defense?"

"I don't know." Though she was staring down at the crusty roll she held, she didn't seem to realize she was pulling it into tiny shreds.

Malone reached across the table to still her fingers. "Joss. Talk."

Joss took a deep breath and dusted the crumbs from her hands. "My dad was a brush track trainer. There wasn't a lot of money in that, but we always had food on the table and laughter. There was always laughter. Daddy could've made more going out on the oil rigs, but he always said he'd rather be home with us and eat beans than gone half the time just so we could eat steak. He taught me to ride, and I was good. I made money after school every day exercising racehorses."

Those memories lightened her face for a few minutes before she dropped her gaze. "Then mama got sick. Real sick, real fast. She died of cancer in the spring, and a few months later daddy was hit head-on by a drunk driver in the wrong lane. Daddy was pulling a trailer with four good racehorses. They all died. So did my dad."

Malone felt her heart break for Joss. She was a young girl, still dealing with the grief of losing both parents within months of each other. And, then, somehow, something even worse had happened to her. Someone had failed to keep her safe. "Keep going," she said softly.

"I tried to get emancipation papers. One of the racehorse owners who used my dad as trainer said he'd hire me on full time, but the judge said I was a ward of the state and needed to be in school. I was put in a couple different foster homes. I was at the last one maybe a couple of months before I went to bed one night and woke up the next day lying wedged in some kind of semi-trailer with my duffle bag of clothes and four other girls."

Joss paused to gulp air. Sweat beaded on her forehead. "I started screaming, and the other girls begged me to be quiet so we wouldn't all be killed. I could see daylight through the cracks in the plate metal above me, places it was worn through. It was inches above my face."

There was no doubt the girl was describing a false bottomed floor. For a moment, Malone felt as if they were in the room alone. A kind of white noise filled her ears, filtering out the conversation of other diners, of servers taking orders or refilling drinks. Reaching across the table, she took Joss's hand, almost surprised when Joss gripped hers in turn. Joss had been cautious of being touched, never reaching out, never stepping into the occasional light hug that Malone had given.

"That's why you won't sleep in the bed space of the trailer." Though the mattress was king size with plenty of room for two or even three, in a pinch, a person had to sit with care of their head touching the ceiling. Joss preferred the far less comfortable sleeper couch.

Joss shuddered. "I rolled off the nasty smelling blankets so I could breathe. And so there'd be more space between me and the floor above." She spoke in a tone empty of anything she had been feeling then, might be feeling now. "The oldest girl—Carmen—said I'd been drugged. Like them. And I'd probably been given too much. She thought I was going to die before I woke up. All I knew was that I was sick as a dog."

Hearing what Joss had been through, Malone felt ill herself. She fought the bile that crept up her throat.

"I wanted to claw my hair out. It was hard, hard to keep from screaming. Carmen kept talking to me, low and quiet until I could think again. We made a plan. She said we'd be let out every few hours to pee in the bushes, always in some field or dirt road. One guy would hold a gun on us. The driver always stayed in the truck. Carmen kept telling the other girls to say nothing. All they had to do was get out of the truck and just say nothing. I could tell she was worried they'd mess it up, being so much younger and scared and all."

Malone wasn't sure she wanted an answer to what she was about to ask. "How old were they?"

"Carmen was eighteen. The other girls were younger than me, maybe twelve or thirteen."

She'd been right. Better not to have known that there were two young girls on their own somewhere with no way to find them now. She nodded for Joss to go on.

"I was the tallest, and we figured I was probably also the strongest of us, so the next time the truck stopped and the three were allowed to climb out, Carmen told him I was still out cold. It was close to dark by then, which was good." Joss stopped for a moment.

She took another deep breath. "Being still when that trap door was opened was harder than I thought it would be. Carmen had said I should make sure all three of them were out before I moved, so he wouldn't be looking in. That she'd take her time in the weeds. My knees were shaky when I climbed out of that hole, some from fear, but I knew I was weaker than I thought from whatever they gave me. I was scared, but I was desperate. The guy had his back to me, keeping an eye on the other girls, when I took a running jump from the back of that truck. I aimed for his head. It was a long way down, farther than I expected it to be. I guess he heard me because he turned at the last minute. He saw me, but he didn't have time to move. I don't know what he hit when he fell, but he didn't get up. That's where I got all the bruises. I crashed into him hard, as hard as I could. I knew if I didn't, I'd never get away."

She pulled her hand back from Malone's to take a long drink from her glass of ice water.

"He saw me," she repeated.

"What matters is you got away from him, from them."

"Carmen had said we should run in different directions. The men might catch up with one of us, two if the men decided to split up looking, but we'd all at least have a chance at getting away. Carmen and the two younger ones scattered, but I went just far enough into the woods to find a good tree and climbed it. I knew I could sit quiet for hours if I had to, and I wanted to stay close to the dirt road we were on. At least it would lead somewhere."

"Did any of the girls get away?"

"All three, as far as I know. I hope they're somewhere safe. When the driver got out, I heard him cussing when he found the man with the gun laid out on the ground. A few minutes later, I heard him throw stuff out of the back of the trailer and pull out. I suspected he'd left the other guy right where he found him. I knew I couldn't wait long in case he wasn't dead and managed to get up so I climbed out of that tree. I was scared to death, but I wanted my clothes and the little bit of money I had tucked into a seam of the duffle bag so long ago I don't remember why. Sure enough, the guy was still lying right where I landed on him. I didn't get any closer than I had to, but he didn't move. I grabbed my bag from the pile of blankets we'd been laying on and started walking. The truck wasn't really parked in the woods, like I'd thought. Just beside a thin line of trees. Not too far past that was a parking area full of trucks and trailers."

With that Joss leaned back in her chair, watching Malone with wary eyes.

"The rodeo. Where you climbed aboard my trailer."

Joss nodded cautiously.

"You were brave. It must have been very, very hard to get back in a small, enclosed space."

Without speaking, Joss nodded again.

"You were also very, very lucky that the trailer was mine." Her mind circled back to Joss's first comment. "What is it you need help to do? Find out if the guy lived?"

"No. I don't care. I didn't mean to kill him, but I don't care if he's dead or alive. But the foster parents ... I think they sold me. I went to sleep in the room they said was mine and woke up in a truck. Someone needs to know so they can't do it again."

Malone felt a slow rage simmering in the pit of her stomach and wished she hadn't eaten before hearing what Joss had been put through. The girl's story explained why there had been no Amber Alert for Joss. Her disappearance had probably been documented as another runaway. If it even had been reported. She had no idea how often agencies checked in with foster parents. "I'll help you, Joss. And I'll keep you safe. Even if I have to lay someone out on the ground."

Joss smiled faintly, looking far less tense now that she had placed her problem with an adult she trusted. "I'll bet you could, too."

In that moment, Malone knew if she never succeeded again at anything in her life, she would succeed at the promise she'd just made. Joss was counting on her and looking at her with such confidence it was almost scary.

"Do you think you could help me get emancipation papers?"

"We can work on that when we get done in Montgomery." But where Malone's mind truly went with Joss's question wasn't setting her up as an adult who had to make her own way. Joss needed a parent, at least one, who cared about her well-being, and Malone wouldn't be the first single person to adopt. "There are attorneys I trust back home in Georgia."

Home. As she said the word, Malone realized that somewhere along the miles, she'd made another decision as well.

* * *

Three hours later, Malone sat astride Jaz and watched Joss canter Gemini in ever-tightening circles. The fine-boned mare tended to be hyper and the corkscrew workout, starting big and easing her in toward the center with a steady hand on the rein, tended to settle her. Malone had learned early on if she started with smaller circles the mare fought continually for more room and more speed. Joss took instructions well and learned quickly. Which reminded Malone that Joss needed to be in school. Her future could be as bright as any other teen. Maybe homeschool if she chose to stay with Malone, then college. But they couldn't get her registered for anything until the mess that had happened to her was straightened out and, hopefully, people were in prison for what they'd done.

Maybe a name change with adoption would be safest for her. No one would ever need to know that the girl who had disappeared from south Louisiana was safe with her.

"Malone."

She turned, startled, realizing that her name had been spoken for a second time.

"Nick. I'm sorry. I was lost in thought."

Nick stepped up on the lowest rung of the tall pipe fence that enclosed the practice pen and crossed his arms along the top. "That girl is a better hand than most of the young men I have on my payroll. I might try to steal her away from you."

"She's younger than she looks, and I have to return her to her family at the end of the week but, you're right. Joss is an awesome talent, and I'll miss her." Malone wasn't much for lying, but Joss's safety depended upon there being no possibility of an indiscreet word here or there. And cowboys, so taciturn in movie land, were, in reality, very good at gossip. She and Joss had agreed to a story, and Malone would hold firm.

A glance at Nick's face told Malone his thoughts weren't really on Joss and her skill with a horse. His next words proved it. "I can't figure out what the hell is going on around here, Malone. I'm hearing whispers here and there, that Quinn's death may not have been accidental."

Malone turned her gaze back to Joss so that her face was slightly tilted away from Nick. She wasn't good at subterfuge. "Surely that can't be true. There were a dozen or so people working those chutes. You know the association—Cade—is super careful that the workers aren't short-handed anywhere. There're enough hazards with what all of us do every day to be careless in the handling of an event. And why would anyone want to hurt Quinn?"

"I'm not saying it's true, but ... there's talk."

"I haven't heard anything, but Joss and I got away from the grounds for several hours this morning. We needed some breathing room after all that has happened." Two days, two deaths. She hesitated, but Cade would need to know what rumors were floating. "What kind of talk?"

Nick sighed. "That maybe something wasn't right with his bull rope. Maybe it wasn't secure. Hell, I don't know."

"It was his rope, wasn't it?"

"Yeah, his cousin picked it up after."

"Did anything look odd about it?"

"No. But ... one of the flank men said Quinn's expression changed right as the bull made his first leap out of the chute. Said it went from his usual daredevil 'I've got this' to real fear. The guy's swearing something went wrong, and Quinn knew it."

"Maybe something did. Or maybe Quinn got careless this once." Malone spoke softly sensing that Nick was truly upset by what had happened. They all were. But every cowboy carried his own rope and helped those working the chutes secure it around the bull. The gate wasn't opened until they gave the nod. "The bull was one of yours?"

"Yeah." Nick pushed away from the fence. "Mine."

"That doesn't make you responsible for what happened in that chute, Nick. Just like the owners of the horses I ride aren't responsible if I get hurt or killed while riding or handling them."

His expression didn't ease, and she felt truly bad for him. He gave her a strained smile. "You be careful out there tonight. I won't wish you luck. You don't need it. Malone, you're one of the best—to my mind, *the best*—out here this week, but I am wishing you real success. I'll be watching."

For the first time, Malone wondered if the look in his eyes that she'd always passed off as pure flirtation wasn't something more than that. Watching him walk away, she hoped not. She'd rather see his attentions turned solidly elsewhere—heaven knew there were plenty of women who'd had their eyes on him over the last few years—but Malone only ever thought of him with friendship. Nick was everything most single women would want in a man. But Malone didn't want the complication or the risk of a man in her life. And, if she ever decided she did, Nick wasn't going to be the one.

As Joss rode up to the fence, Malone pulled her gaze away from Nick's departure.

"That guy's after you," Joss said knowingly.

"I'm sorry for that," Malone said sincerely. "I'm not in

the market."

"Not for him."

Malone decided some comments were best left unanswered, and she nudged Jaz into a walk. But she didn't miss Joss's knowing look as she made her escape.

Chapter 17

Cade walked into the show office and immediately noticed the new face. Detective Armand, he supposed. He gave her a quick nod and walked past the counter, into his office. To his surprise, she followed.

She stood with her back to the doorway, one step inside. Cade realized at once that she had placed herself where she could be seen as not approaching him but couldn't be heard by any casual listener. He studied her for a moment, realizing she had features that could be highlighted to real beauty but had somehow been downplayed by makeup. Interesting.

"Riverstock's fiancée asked for the bell off his bull rope, said she'd had it engraved with both their names inside after he asked her to marry him. The family let her have it. She was pleased—heartbroken—but pleased to get it back."

Cade didn't ask how she knew all that. Ryder had said she was good at her job. "And the rope with the severed handhold?"

"The locals are sharing information for now but not going public with it. Plain bell, no engraving."

"So not his rope."

"Not his rope. But Ryder is convinced it's the one that was on that bull when the chute opened. Marchmann is halfway to believing. Give me a task I can take back out front."

He looked at her blankly for a minute then nodded as he realized her meaning. "Flowers and a card with every staff member's signature need to be sent to Riverstock's family." He'd done the same for Roland Walker though the circumstances had been far different.

She nodded and walked out. Her voice carried back to his office. "Mr. Delaney said flowers need to be sent to the cowboy's family. Everyone needs to sign the card. I'll go get a card. I don't know how to order flowers or what to get, but I'll figure it out."

With that she strolled through the front door, for all the world like a student intern who hadn't a clue about office etiquette.

Cade's amusement at her tactics faded. He rocked back in his chair and stared at his steepled fingers, picturing again Dawson White's face as he'd looked at the rope in his hand. Without a doubt, his expression had registered confusion. Was he trying to understand why a rope in perfect condition had failed the rider? Or was he wondering why the rope handed to him showed no sign of the sabotage he knew should exist?

What had Callahan seen in the moments before Quinn had signaled the gatemen to throw the chute wide with a dip of his head? Some sleight of hand and fast exchange?

Or was it as simple as Quinn misjudging his readiness or the gatemen misjudging some movement for the nod that he was ready? And if that were true, whose was the rope with the half-severed hand braid?

Cade wished he could ask Callahan that question. Even as the thought came to him, he shook his head. He wasn't quite crazy enough to think a cat could find a way to answer. Or was he?

* * *

Malone doesn't talk enough. I can't always tell when I need to follow her and when I need to be about my own business. I'm most comfortable when she and Joss remain together, but Joss is grooming horses with Luke to keep her company, and Malone is off on some mission.

I slip into the show office on her heels, then into Cade's office as she hesitates in the open doorway. Cade is engrossed in what appears to be a report of some sort. I see columns of numbers so likely financial information for this rodeo business he manages.

Malone is safe here, but there are times the information my humans carry in their head could be of real help. Getting them to share can be a challenge. Maybe someday, in the distant future, they'll evolve to the same level of unspoken communication as cats. For now, I'm forced to find ways to hear what I need to know. I leap to my usual comfortable spot in the wide-ledge of the window sill as she taps at the doorframe.

"Cade?"

"Malone." *Cade stands, ever the gentleman.* "Come in."

He doesn't sit until she takes a seat. I've learned enough to know that he came up through the rodeo ranks as a team roper, so either these contestants are not all as rough and tumble as they've appeared to be in my time here or he has gained significant polish in the years he's been in the business end of the sport. It's a sport that has mostly excluded women, and I wonder if that will change in the years to come.

"Do you have a moment?"

"A lifetime if you want it."

If I were human, I'd roll my eyes at that response. I'm not surprised when Malone blinks, then opens and closes her mouth before finally saying, "It's about Joss." *She must see concern in Cade's expression because she hastily adds,* "She's okay. At least for now. It's a long story."

He rises and walks to the door to close it to a mere slit of an opening. "That's Aleta's signal to run interference with anyone wanting to see me." *I win a bet with myself when he doesn't return to the chair behind his desk but takes the one next to Malone. They're now close enough to touch. It will be interesting to see if either makes that move.*

Time enough for speculations later. I have a feeling Malone is about to impart the type of news I need.

"Is Joss upset with what has been going on around here?"

"No, it's nothing to do with that." *She hesitates.* "I think I'm going to need a good lawyer for Joss. I thought you might be able to help."

Not what either of us expected her to say. I'd place a bet on that.

"What has she done?" *I hear concern but no condemnation. Good man.*

And an increasingly angry man as Malone tells Joss's story, an evil story of human greed and cruelty. I've heard of such things but never been close to a case involving human trafficking. An ugly business. Uglier than murder, plain and simple.

Cade listens and comforts and reassures. Even as Malone leaves us to prepare for her evening competition, I suspect she has yet to couple what happened to Joss with what has been happening around us here. But when we are once more alone in that small office, Cade turns his gaze to me, and I gather, like me, he's pieced the picture together. 'Callahan, I need to know who handed Quinn Riverstock the damaged rope you brought to me.'

He rises and takes his hat from the rack, twisting it in his hands for a moment, deep in thought. I can feel the fury strong within him, see it in his eyes. I follow him from the office, out into strong afternoon sunlight.

I know how easy it would be for me to identify the guilty cowboy to him. A leap and pounce upon a leg or back as we stroll the rodeo grounds. But my cooler head cautions me to be more careful than that. The reveal can't be made to an angry man on the hunt for guilt. I don't know that Cade has himself in hand. Cade has a reputation which must be protected for his own good and the good of the association. A fistfight is beneath him, as satisfying as that might be for him to start and me to witness.

For now, I'll follow, not lead. If our path leads to the bucking chutes and cowboy Dawson, at some point, I'll have to decide then, what to do and how to do it.

* * *

Well, Cade thought, it's a start … Malone turning to him for help. He'd wondered more than once in the hours since they'd stood together on that sidewalk, wondered if he'd only imagined Malone's brief response to his embrace, his kiss, wondered what she'd been feeling since. He'd dared a lot in that moment, and all he'd really known was that she hadn't pulled away, walked away. But that one brief moment hadn't been enough and he suspected it never would.

The first night of the competition, he'd been waiting for her at the end of the alley. But Tyge had stepped in ahead of him, a reminder of all the years the cowboy had been there for her and Cade had not. The two had never noticed Cade as they'd passed by deep in conversation. He'd been jealous, hell he still was. But she'd come to him now. He'd let her down once, but he'd be damned if he ever would again.

Cade hadn't a clue how or where to begin in connecting Joss's tragic story to the murder of two rough stock riders, but he couldn't shake a feeling, a strong feeling, the connection was there. Ryder was looking for traffickers. Cade's mind had jumped to drugs, perhaps even guns, particularly in today's political clime. But humans? With people he knew, perhaps intimately, as friends and comrades and business associates?

The thought disgusted him, but the facts were strong. Cade couldn't believe it coincidental that the truck carrying Joss and three other girls had been stopped in close proximity to the Lake Charles rodeo, perhaps even on the rodeo grounds themselves. Couldn't find it coincidental that Ryder was looking here, at the rodeo crowd. Ryder had more than hinted that he thought stock trailers, whether for bulls or broncs or calves or steers, were a possible means of illicit transportation.

It wasn't a big leap to look at potential connections

between those two things and the murders of Roland Walker and Quinn Riverstock. And Cade was now firmly convinced that Riverstock's death was no accident.

He wondered if agreeing to move the Southeastern Circuit Finals here had been a terrible mistake. His mistake. Sometimes what looked too good to be true was just that. Too good to be true. But the deal presented to the association had meant more payout money for the finalists and more savings in the future.

He'd been offered the year-old facility—all inclusive, from coliseum to barns to outside working pens to city hookups for trailers—at a fraction of what the cost would have been. The benefit to the city was a five-year contract, with the agreement that the association would continue to use the facility each of those years at a reduced cost. During those five years, if either the city or the association failed to show a solid profit, the contract could be ended by written notification. At the end of five years, it could be extended, renegotiated, or allowed to lapse.

The board of directors had been enthusiastic once they'd had time to review the potential numbers. Cade had been pleased. Theirs wasn't the largest or oldest Pro-Rodeo Association, but it was growing by leaps and bounds. Cade was glad to contribute to that growth. But he hadn't anticipated murder in the mix, not one, much less two. Now he had to keep his wits about him and, with the help of an unusual gray cat, find out who was behind the deaths and if the crimes were as connected to Ryder's investigation and Joss's story as he thought. And knowing he was counting on a cat to help him do all that made him doubtful how much he had left of his wits to keep about him.

Cade started on the fringes of the grounds, just walking, looking, and thinking. He felt a little conspicuous with Callahan weaving in and out between him and Townsend. The first cold front of the season had made for a chill and dreary start to the event but left glorious fall weather in its wake. The brilliant blue of the sky and the warmth of the sun seemed at odds with the grimness of his mood. He had to work at a pleasant expression as he greeted his members and their families.

He stopped to watch Brax working with a couple of little britches ropers, helping them roll up their ropes and guiding their swings so that one finally looped the horns on the roping dummy and let out a whoop of exultation. Luke sat in a folding chair half watching, half working rosin into his own rope.

Luke looked up, watchful, undoubtedly expecting more bad news of some sort.

Cade smiled, sorry that events had conspired to make a generally happy-go-lucky young man so cautious. "Congratulations on your winnings last night. You and your dad pulled a good check."

Some of the stiffness left Luke's shoulders. "We needed it. Not the money, so much, you know. But the win."

Cade did know. A couple of other teams, equally talented and with even more experience, had had poor luck and a slow start which was proving a drag on them now. He couldn't say why adversity made some dig in and some lose heart.

When he would have walked on, Luke spoke again, softly. "Mr. Delaney?"

"Yeah?"

"What's happening here?"

Cade wished he had an answer for that, at least a better one than all he could offer. "Whatever it is, I know there are two different law enforcement agencies teamed up to find the answer." Teamed up was probably overstating reality but no need for Luke or anyone else to know that. "Just focus on your riding and your throw, Luke."

"Some of the other guys are getting scared one of us will be next, but I don't think whatever's happening has anything to do with us or the rodeo. Not really."

Luke watched Cade carefully, clearly hoping for affirmation of his belief from someone he trusted, someone in authority, someone who'd know if he had reason to be afraid. Cade felt out of his element in one sense, but confident in another. Watching out for his members, as well as creating a calm environment, was a key component of his position.

"I think you're right, Luke. Still, be careful of your surroundings so that you aren't caught up in something you don't mean or need to be, but otherwise I believe you're all safe enough." As safe as anyone could be. For decades, Montgomery hadn't been considered the safest city in the United States, but things were changing dramatically with the revitalization projects going on. This facility newly built. Restaurants and theatres opening. Strip malls disappearing and burglar bars being removed from storefront windows. Progress, slow but sure.

He clapped Luke reassuringly on the shoulder as he moved on.

Brax gave him a nod and a wave, but didn't take his close attention off the two youngsters in front of him.

Near the first barn, he passed a group of teenage girls in blue jeans and sneakers, carrying multiple shopping bags, many bearing the names of their sponsors for the week. Good for business. A group of teenage boys trailed behind them, but as one of the girls tossed a comment with a name attached over her shoulder, he stayed relaxed. He supposed boys the world over tagged along with girls on a shopping mission.

A man in jeans and boots stood propped against the side of the first barn. Cade hesitated. The jeans were not faded, and the boots were unscathed by barn work. Not a scuff mark anywhere. He could have been a fan or a parent or merely a passerby were it not for the look in his eyes. The sport coat wasn't out of place in the late October weather. Still.

Cade looked for, but didn't see, the tell-tale bulge of a concealed carry. Even so, he went on his own intuition and the sudden interest Callahan displayed in the man.

Stopping in front of him, Cade held out his hand. "Badge."

"Mr. Delaney, you need to walk on."

"Bull shit. Ryder can go to hell if he thinks he's planting people on these grounds without my knowing." He had to guess between Marchmann and Ryder but suspected the locals didn't have the funding to spot extra officers for investigative purposes.

The lawman scowled as he passed his badge over for scrutiny. "Ryder won't be pleased."

"By what?" Cade commented affably. "By you not having sense enough to wear faded jeans and old boots if you wanted to blend in here? This is a private facility and under my control for the duration of this event. You're here at my discretion or not at all."

"That wouldn't hold up in court."

Cade grinned although it probably looked more like a baring of teeth than humor. "Probably not, but Ryder would be even less pleased if it ended up there, don't you think?"

When the undercover agent gave a grudging nod, Cade handed his badge back to him and moved on. Though he wondered if there were others elsewhere on the grounds, he didn't see much use in questioning Ryder's man. He wasn't likely to get an answer, at least not a straightforward one.

On the other hand, the man's presence could well be a bargaining chip. Joss needed help, and Ryder likely had strings to tug that could provide that help. He placed a quick call, and Ryder answered on the first ring. Cade made quick work of telling the marshal that he was in Cade's debt for not running off his man and even quicker work of telling him that every favor should be reciprocated. Ryder agreed to talk with Joss after the evening performance.

Assured of Ryder's cooperation, Cade called Malone who wasn't enthusiastic about the suggestion but promised to reassure Joss as best she could that this was a good thing. And Joss, after all, was the one who had asked to do something positive.

Cade's thoughts and long stride carried him closer and closer to the area where stock contractors parked their trailers after unloading. In his heart he couldn't believe that any of the contractors he'd worked with, shared meals with, lifted an occasional beer with, could be involved in the ugliness happening around him. But there were newcomers, and some of the old-timers had stepped back as their offspring—sons and daughters both—stepped forward to take over the business. For the most part, those who were here he knew and trusted. But they supplied the larger venues, where the payouts were bigger and the money paid for stock was reflective of the caliber animal. Smaller or newer districts, like the one in Lake Charles used the minor, more local contractors. But no one had died in Lake Charles. They were dying *here*.

Regardless, Cade wanted to look at some actual stock trailers, think back to those he and his father had run, how they had been built, how they might have been modified to conceal. His effort might tell him nothing, but grasping at straws was better than grasping at thin air.

The area was virtually bare of anything but empty trucks and trailers. The sounds from around the arena and paddock areas came to him muted. Some distance away, two women held horses on lead ropes, talking quietly as they let the animals graze on the narrow strip of lush grass between the paved parking and the fence that backed the city street beyond.

Cade walked slowly between the long, empty trailers. From time to time, he stooped to examine the various undercarriages of the trailers, pondering possibilities for concealed compartments, how one could be constructed on this or that trailer design. It wouldn't be impossible to create, but how easily could it be camouflaged from the DOT officers who patrolled weigh stations? Occasionally, Callahan would leap lightly to a wheel fender as if peering inside. Each time Townsend would whine faintly until the cat returned to the pavement. In silence, Cade noted the professional logos etched with the names of the various contractors.

Dossett Inc., run by Gaylon Dossett and his wife, who was as short and round as Gaylon himself, hauled some of the best broncs in the business, to Cade's mind. He felt guilty thinking about using Carlisle Contracting in their place next year, but Dossett had raised his rates steadily and significantly over the last few years. Cade had questioned him, pushed him on it, but Dossett hadn't backed down on his pricing, and it didn't appear likely he would. Rodeo was a business, and if Carlisle could produce comparable stock at a more equitable price, Cade wouldn't have much choice.

Andrews and Sons. Nick always swore that if he couldn't stock quality bulls, he wouldn't stock at all. Cade had never known him to disappoint. Nick hadn't had it easy the past few years, but with his sons taking more and more of the business, the lines of stress had seemed to be easing each time Cade saw him these days.

Carriere Steers was based in Little Rock. The company wasn't quite a newcomer but still the most recent addition to the lineup. They carried some of the finest bull dogging steers in the United States. Cade had vetted them thoroughly before taking them on and, so far, they hadn't disappointed.

The last of the rigs belonged to Jemson Ventures. Lang Jemson had graduated with a veterinary degree, worked in the profession for five years and walked away without a backward glance to partner with his father-in-law on supplying roping calves to local rodeo. It was a family-owned business with a pristine reputation, and the wives of the two men were as invested in the business as their husbands. Cade couldn't see them involved in wrong-doing.

Hell, he couldn't see any of them caught up in something so unsavory. With every step forward, he felt more and more like a traitor to the team who supported the association. Because with every step forward, he wondered, just wondered, if it were a possibility. He thought of the decade he and his father hauled calves to rodeos, how he would have felt if anyone had been looking at their rig with such thoughts at the back of their mind.

Callahan waited for him and Townsend on the hood of the last Jemson truck, looking bored. If there had been anything out of the way to find, the cat would have found it. Cade had given up pretending he thought otherwise. Townsend yipped softly and wagged his tail as he stared up at the cat until Callahan leapt down to give him a supercilious glance before leading the way back in the direction they'd come.

Cade's cell phone buzzed as he crossed in front of the coliseum. He glanced at the name and sighed.

"Good afternoon, Jo. What's up?" Other than her worries—and his—about how murder might impact the terms of their contract. He'd known Joanne Legier long before she became part of the management team for Montgomery's new equine facility. She'd traded on their friendship when she contacted him with the possibility of a deal between the city and the Rodeo Association.

"Cade, do you have time to join me for a drink and a few minutes to talk?"

He'd rather have put this off but … "I do if it's close and brief. I can't be far or away long during the performances." Particularly not in light of the events of the past two days.

"I'm leaving my office. I'll pick you up in ten minutes and bring you right back as soon as you say the word, I promise."

"I'll be in front of the coliseum box office."

He left Townsend with Aleta, realizing that Callahan had disappeared on him somewhere along the way. Joanne slid her sports car to a skillful stop, smiling as she got out. She greeted him with the hug of a longstanding relationship that had survived several transitions and emerged as something less than she'd made clear she wanted and something more than he once would've thought possible.

"Want to drive?" she asked with a grin as she caught him admiring her car.

He caught the keys she tossed to him. It wasn't a car he had any desire to own, but he was a red-blooded male. Handling the sleek power under that hood was an offer he wouldn't turn down.

* * *

"Who's that?" Joss watched with quiet curiosity on her face as Cade slid behind the wheel of an electric blue car.

Malone glanced across at the couple she'd been pretending not to notice as she and Joss walked out of the show office. "Her name used to be Joanne Ellis. They dated in college." And she still wore her hair short, framing perfect features. And she was still looked more than attractive in clothes too cute to be warm.

"Does she run barrels?"

"Not that I know, but I do, and we have a lot to do before then." To her relief, Joss took the hint and turned the conversation to the horses and the tasks ahead of them.

Chapter 18

With a glass of wine in front of each of them, Cade listened while Joanne made small talk. A local talent played light jazz with a soft touch on a keyboard. Another time he probably would have appreciated both the entertainment and the mood lighting. As it was, he had to tamp back his impatience. He'd realized during their initial meetings regarding the change in venue for the district finals that Joanne hadn't changed much since college. She still took her time getting to the point in any conversation. Unlike Malone.

The simple thought of her made him anxious to get back to the rodeo grounds.

Cade took a sip of the wine he rarely drank and wished he'd ordered beer. But he wasn't going to be there long enough for it to matter. He was unlikely to finish his drink in any case.

"What's on your mind, Jo?"

She turned her glass by the stem without lifting it from the table. Her dark eyes looked anxious, and he waited for whatever bad news she had to impart. "You've had a bit of publicity the last few days."

"And little of it good," he stated baldly without offering any excuses. They might as well get to the point of her conversation.

"But one was an accident," she offered. "I mean it's horrible, but it happens in any high-risk sport, right?"

He looked at her, surprised at her direction. He nodded. "Yeah. It happens." He wasn't about to enlighten her that Riverstock's death was likely *not* an accident.

"And the other. It could have been a fight that got out of hand. I mean, the police don't *know* at this point, do they?"

"If they know, they aren't telling me."

"So, it likely could have happened anywhere? Any other city you might have been in if you weren't here," she pressed.

Cade leaned back in his chair. This was definitely taking a different track than the one he'd thought she'd embark on. He'd expected to be castigated for the Rodeo Association marring the new image the city was striving to create. But, business being business, Cade decided to press his advantage. "Maybe." He paused intentionally. "But, Jo, I've been in rodeo since my teens. This is a first for me. I've had cowboys tear up bars before, cut each other with pocket knives, hit each other with barstools, get bones broken and need stitches. I haven't had anyone murdered on the grounds."

Her chin dropped. "Yeah." She spoke the word softly, then straightened her shoulders. "Well, I want you to know that I've met with the police chief, and he understands that this simply can't happen again. They'll need to do a better job patrolling the area around the equine center. I've put a lot—a lot!—into this deal with you. And, Cade, it's paying off! The hoteliers and restaurateurs are already calling me about the dates for next year, wanting to time other attractions with it, target their approach."

Cade felt more than a little guilty for her distress, particularly knowing what he knew and suspecting what he suspected. In all probability, the association had brought this trouble with them. But there was nothing he could say that didn't carry the potential to jeopardize Ryder's investigation and keep girls like Joss at risk. He wouldn't take that chance, regardless.

"I appreciate your talking with them. I'd like to see this resolved sooner rather than later. I have a whole lot of nervous competitors. I need to know they're comfortable coming back next year. They need to know they'll be safe."

He didn't intend to cause Joanne the tension he saw in her expression, but that was as honest as anything he could offer. Regardless of the outcome of the investigation, regardless of who was arrested, what had happened needed resolution for all of them. The less than honest part was that Cade really didn't think the city police were going to be the ones to solve this case.

He glanced at the time as Joanne dropped him off close to where she'd picked him up, relieved that they'd been gone barely an hour. Aleta would have called if anything ominous had happened in his absence.

Collecting Townsend from the show office, he headed

to the coliseum, giving a brief thought to Callahan's whereabouts while knowing the cat was independent and self-sufficient to say the least.

* * *

Although I don't think our time was wasted in perusing the stock trailers, I also don't necessarily think it garnered us any new information. I know it didn't give me an opportunity to reveal the identity of the cowboy who sent Quinn Riverstock to his death. Frustrating, that. I'm not certain, and certainly can't prove, that he damaged that bull rope, but I'm convinced beyond reasonable doubt that he knew the damage existed and what the consequences could be. That makes him guilty of something.

To that end, I need to gather up Cade who should, by now, have returned from his joyride with a pretty lady in a speedy car and maneuver him to the bucking chutes where we're most likely to encounter that cowboy. I've checked the show office, and Townie is no longer ensconced there so I've no doubt they're on the grounds together someplace. I also strongly suspect that he's sought the presence of Malone so, first stop, the barn area where she'll be readying for tonight's barrel race.

All things considered I'd better be on full alert as I cross that distance. So many occurrences in such short order make it critical that I don't miss a lick, whether it seems of immediate interest or not.

The sport of rodeo sure does pull a crowd and generates an amazing sense of energy. Morning is lightest in terms of spectators and interest, but the crowd increases throughout the day and peaks each evening when the barrel racing and rough stock riding takes place.

I move lightly among the coming and going of fans, young parents pushing strollers, children tugging at the hands of their parents, adults navigating the elderly in wheelchairs or walking slowly beside them as they maneuver their walkers. Rodeo, it seems, appeals to all ages. I find the sport interesting, but I'm not overly fond of the clowns, outside their role of bull fighters. Now that I find intriguing. Their skill and courage astound me. Then, disappointingly, they descend into the ignoble depths of loud noises and inept comedy routines that—for some reason—delight the crowds.

I see a familiar face, but an unhappy one. Nick Andrews looks to be squared off with his son. Typically, I avoid familial arguments. Too messy. But something about their expressions draws me closer though I decide to remain beyond their notice. That distance, unfortunately, means I can't hear the words of either though expressions tell me every one of those words is being spoken in anger. The younger Andrews pulls a thick wad of bills from the pocket of his jeans and hands it across to his elder. Perhaps money borrowed and unwillingly returned. Humans don't seem to know how to push offspring from the nest when it's time. Cats are smarter in that regard. We're cared for until we can care for ourselves, then we're sent to make our mark on the world.

The younger man stalks away after the exchange, leaving his father to stare after him in sorrow and disappointment and, yes, clear concern. Humans. Interesting but altogether illogical.

Malone is exactly where I expected her to be, brushing a lovely blue roan to a high gloss. I'm fond of the color of this one's coat perhaps because it stands out in a world of bays and sorrels, rather like a gray cat in a bunch of tabbies.

Joss is busy with the scrubbing and filling of water buckets, a never-ending chore, I've learned.

There's no sign of Cade, so I suppose he's tied up in the running of things, a necessary task that can't be left to just anyone.

Joss moves to stand in the open doorway of the stall, watching Malone. "How do you ride this one?"

I would've thought that an odd question if I hadn't become so savvy with barrel speak. I'll even confess I might once have answered in my head with a tone of scorn that the horse would be ridden astride with saddle as they all are.

"Frisco runs to the left which is always tricky for me. I have to be careful that I don't pull him off point. He's also a push-style so I can't sit too quick, not nearly as early as most of the others. If I do, he'll slow too soon. If I ride him right at the next rodeo, he'll pull a check." *Malone stops grooming to look fully at Joss, giving her a smile.* "If I don't pull a check, you can ask me what I did wrong." *She clearly intends for Joss to stay with her in the long term.*

Joss smiles back at her. "I won't have to."

Her faith in Malone is complete. And understandable.

They move to the next stall where, soon, Malone has the horse named Jaz saddled and ready. Joss retrieves her western hat from its hook in the stall they have set up as a temporary tack and feed room. It keeps everything they need close at hand for the care of the horses. Along we go to the warmup pen, while I keep my eyes peeled for Cade. I don't entirely understand my own rising tension, but I have an increasing sense of foreboding as if time and opportunity were slipping away. Though unexplained by anything I've seen or heard through the day, I've learned not to ignore those feelings. Something, just below the surface, is unsettling me.

Time is critical and action must be taken. Why and what action, I'll have to figure out as I go.

As Joss follows Malone, I veer off, more determined than ever to find Cade and give him the information he needs, the information that he asked of me. The identity of the cowboy who handed Riverstock the rope that failed with the bull's first twist and turn out of the shoot.

* * *

Cade was determined to be waiting when Malone left the arena this time, and he'd be damned if he'd yield one inch to Tyge LaMonte. He almost hoped the other guy would dare just so he could plant him one. And wouldn't that be the icing on the cake for a man who was supposed to be an example for his members. A good example.

Hell. He was losing it. He made a brief stop at the concession stand where he was handed a bottle of chilled water, and his money was declined because he was recognized. Oh, yeah, it'd be real wise of him to get into a fistfight with LaMonte.

Just as he'd decided to take a seat in the stands for a few minutes, he saw Callahan prowling the broad crowd-thronged hallway. He stopped to see which way the cat was headed when Callahan turned and looked him in the eyes. Without hesitation, the cat wove his way through the cowboy boots and sneakers around him never taking his eyes off Cade.

When Callahan reached Cade, he didn't stop but continued on, glancing back once to be sure Cade followed. Cade did.

Callahan led him without hesitation to the bucking chutes where the first bronc rider was limping in painful victory from the arena. He'd made his ride, now he'd be praying his points would be worth the pain of the landing. Cade heard the announcer call his score as he rounded the corner. It was a good one. He felt certain the cowboy had heard as well, judging by the grin on his face.

Cade felt a sense of urgency to complete whatever Callahan's mission might be and make his way to the other end of the arena before Malone's run.

While the bronc riders were competing for their

moment of glory, the bull riders were warming up with stretches and making last minute checks on their equipment. Only the barrel racers stood between them and their event. Nerves were heightened. He heard it in the ribbing each gave the other, saw it in the taut expressions on their faces, in the knee bends and elbow pulls against pipe railing around the livestock enclosures as they tried to work the tension from their muscles.

He followed in Callahan's wake, the gray cat casting glances his way from time to time to ensure obedience. Cade felt a grim sort of amusement at the situation in which he found himself. Amusement faded as he realized who the cat had lined up in his sight.

The cowboy stood propped against the fence, his back to Cade, his bull rope slung over one shoulder, the bell hanging low. If Dawson saw the cat, he gave no evidence of it, even when Callahan moved close enough to touch him. Callahan sat on his haunches and turned one last glance toward Cade before he pushed upward and touched the dangling bell very lightly with extended claw.

Something, the subtle movement of the rope, the tiny swing of the bell, or the light sound of it caught Dawson's attention, pulled it away from conversation with fellow competitors and the tension of knowing his ride was sheer minutes away. He glanced down at the cat, pushed him away.

Cade felt gut-punched as he watched the swing of the bell slowly subside. There were a multitude of things he would have liked to do in that moment. He did none of them.

Dawson turned and his glance met Cade's briefly before he gave an offhand nod and looked back toward the activity in the arena.

Cade now had knowledge but no proof. Without proof, he had no clear path forward. But, with fury rising from the pit of his stomach, he knew he'd find it. As much as he wished for action, there was nothing to be done here or now.

What he couldn't fathom was motive. Sure, they were competitors but so were all of the bull riders drawn to this place and time by their skill, sometimes their luck, and their winnings.

Meeting Callahan's gaze, Cade turned back the way he had come. Halfway around, he heard Malone's name over the loudspeaker and cursed. He'd missed her run. Again.

* * *

I think Cade was less observant in the moment just passed than I could wish. I'm almost positive he failed to see the look of fury I received at bringing attention to our cowboy. How he shielded that fury in the look he gave Cade. Not that Dawson White, by any means, comprehends that my paw on that small brass bell was a well-planned signal, an actual ID of the guilty. Nor would he believe it, if I were able to gloat to him over the fact at any point.

I wish my touch on the bell had been lighter, the bell less easily sounded, even light as it was. If it had been, Dawson White wouldn't have noticed, wouldn't have turned to see Cade.

But when humans are guilty, they're suspicious of everyone and everything. Now, Dawson will wonder why Cade was there in that moment, why he was watching. This exchange, however well intended, may have put Cade at risk.

After all, two are dead. What's one more death to a murderer? Or murderers? Something about his exchange with Quinn, seconds before Riverstock's death, makes me think he's not innocent. But neither do I believe him to be the mastermind behind the breaking of Roland Walker's neck. At least not hands on ... and certainly no pun is intended.

Cade has gone on about his business, but I believe it's in the best interest of the case for me to see where Mr. White goes from here. And who he talks with. We haven't gone far when the sound of footsteps causes me to glance over my shoulder at an unexpected and unwelcome sight.

Why is Tyge following us? Well, maybe not us. I don't think he's even noticed me. But, without a doubt, he's on Dawson's tail. I don't need this complication. Tyge could gum up the works. I haven't completely dissected his role in all of this, but I suspect—for reasons of his own—he's skirting a line between whoever is master villain and the two forces of law now on the case. And a fine, thin line it could prove to be.

I loop back to fall behind him in order to remain unnoticed, but unexpectedly, Tyge veers away. I look up to see what could have alarmed him, but there's nothing more than the usual bunch of cowboys ahead of us. Dawson wades into their midst with the jovial tossing of insults toward the other rough stock riders which repartee I've recognized as a 'stock and trade' for their sport.

After a moment, Dawson maneuvers his way through the cowboys and continues on, which is something of a relief to me. It's late and I'm as tired as I am hungry. Well, perhaps not as tired but close. I endure a lot to help keep the peace around me.

I note a familiar pair as Dawson greets Luke and his father who are walking slowly and seeming lost in talk. I think they fared well in this morning's team-roping competition. It could be they now dissect what they did well and what they think could be improved. I've learned this rehashing is a common practice among rodeo competitors.

Although I expect Dawson to pass them by on whatever mission pulls him, he slows his step and falls into conversation with the father-son team. They draw near the Roberts' trailer, and Luke gives his dad a nod and a smile and goes inside. I'm fascinated by this nomadic lifestyle of rodeo competitors. I can't help but wonder which feels more like a home, these trailers with minute quarters in which they live and travel for weeks, even months on end, or the houses to which they return.

To my surprise, Brax and Dawson prop against the rear bumper of the truck that's unhitched but pulled close to the trailer. It looks as if they're settling in for a good conversation. Feeling more comfortable now that I am among friends or at least friendly acquaintances, I leap lightly to the hood of the truck then on to the cab. Dawson pays me no mind, although Brax casts a curious glance my way before losing interest when I curl into a ball. I'm determined to wait this out until Dawson continues on his way so I may as well take the opportunity to rest a while.

I'm quickly disabused of that notion when Brax glances towards the closed door of the trailer before turning a hard look toward Dawson. "What the hell do you think you're doing?" *His voice is low but as unwelcoming as his expression.*

So much for a friendly chat.

"You worried because your precious son knows we're out here talking?"

'Shut the hell up." *Mr. Roberts no longer looks merely irritated. He's furious, no bones about it. I also detect a bit of apprehension. And there go my good thoughts about Brax Roberts being a decent human being. Something is definitely wrong here.*

'I'll shut up. When I'm ready. You owe me. You owe me a hell of a lot more than you know. But, see, the problem for you is I don't trust you. Ro did. Quinn did. I don't. You need to know that I don't. And, you need to know I've taken out some insurance just in case something happens to me."

'Somebody got overzealous with Roland Walker, I'll admit, but I don't know what the hell you're talking about with Riverstock." *And there is the confession. At least one. I'll admit to being stunned and a bit sickened. This is the father figure I so recently admired?*

'Don't you?" *Dawson's voice is quiet and menacing.* "I did what I had to do, but I blame you. Never forget that."

Clearly the underling believes himself to have the upper hand. And perhaps he does, as the older man pales at his blatant admission of murder.

"You need to get out of here, and if you're smart, you'll disappear for a good long time."

"No can do." *Dawson's expression is almost taunting.* "I'm leading the circuit, right now. Lot of money riding on that—more than what you've paid me the past six months—and I ain't walking away from it. I'm here to let you know that it's best you make sure I come out of all this safe and sound. It won't go well for you—or for your son—if I don't."

Uh-oh, Brax Roberts' complexion has gone flushed rather than ashen. He looks much closer to stroke-city as the younger set of humans might say ... well perhaps not in this rodeo crowd but certainly in the general slang of the day. 'Shut your damn mouth about Luke. He has nothing to do with any of this."

"Well, the way I have it set up in my insurance policy, it sure looks like he does. Remember, if I die or go to jail, you go down and him with you."

Dawson pushes away from his comfortable prop against the tailgate of the truck, but he has one last thing to say. "And that girl Luke's so sweet on?" *I tense at the words. What has this to do with our Joss?* "The one that caught Ro's attention? He wasn't fooling around and let it get out of hand. He said there was something familiar about her, something that made him nervous. He wanted a better look at her. Didn't that last load of girls get away from your drivers at the Lake Charles rodeo? I happen to know that Malone Summers was running that weekend."

Brax is now as taut as I. He stares at Dawson's retreating back as if he'd like to place a sharp blade between those shoulders. I suspect he would if he had a weapon in hand. And if he were not now frightened of whatever Dawson had put in place as insurance for his own safety.

But I don't give a rip for their safety. I have to protect Malone and Joss. I'm going to need Cade's help with this. No doubt about it. I rise slowly and stretch as nonchalantly as I'm able in my current frame of mind. Brax has turned and is staring toward the trailer where his son rests, his expression a mix of fear and frustration. I'm feeling pretty much the same concern for Joss and Malone.

His steps are heavy as he goes inside, and I'm free to leap down to walk along the railing of the truck bed. Just as I prepare to leap again, this time to the pavement below, a glint of moonlight on an object below catches my attention. There, in the bed of the truck, a spur, unbuckled and discarded. A single spur with a narrow inlay of black filigree. And there I have it. The means with which to persuade Cade that a man he's likely known well for half a lifetime isn't worthy of his high regard. Such losses in friendship are always regrettable but sometimes unavoidable, and I don't have a minute of time to waste on lamenting Cade's loss. Joss, and Malone by association, are now in some serious danger.

I turn to go and am startled to realize that Tyge has reappeared. He's in the shadows but visible enough to me. And he's within hearing distance of the exchange between Brax and Dawson. I can't wait to see what he may or may not do with his newfound knowledge. I leave him staring at the door of the Roberts' trailer and beat a path to find Cade.

<h1 style="text-align:center">Chapter 19</h1>

Malone was more than pleased with her run, and Joss was almost vibrating with excitement when she met her in the paddock outside of the arena.

"Oh my gosh, that was awesome. You were flying!"

Malone grinned as she leaned against the mare's neck, breathing in the warm clean scent of horse and victory. "Jaz did her job, and she did it well."

As they made their way back to the barn, Malone's mind slid from her success in the arena to the stress that lay ahead. She pondered how to broach the subject with Joss who, as usual, gave her an easy opening.

"What's wrong?"

"Honestly, nothing, but we do need to talk."

Joss gave a snort of laughter. "I've heard that is the kiss

of death to a relationship."

Malone smiled, glad that Joss had even reached the point of joking after all she'd been through. "Only in the movies or romantic novels. Ours is solid. I've got your back, Joss, I promise." Despite the fact that Joss had expressed a desire to protect other girls from her foster home experience, Malone was worried. Would she panic at the thought of talking with an officer of the law? Decide to run? The mere possibility sent a wave of anxiety through Malone.

"Now you're really worrying me."

"You worry me all the time." Malone gave her a hug and was pleased when Joss didn't stiffen. "You said you wanted to do something about your foster parents. Do you still?"

"Almost more than anything," Joss said fiercely.

Later, Malone thought. *Later I'll ask what she wants more than anything without the almost.* "Cade has arranged for a U.S. Marshal to talk with you. He can help." She hesitated. "But, Joss, if you want to call it off all you have to do is say so. This is your choice. I swear I don't think I could handle it if I woke up and you were just gone. Don't do that to me, okay?" Her eyes stung, but she didn't allow tears to fall. When had this young stowaway become such a vital part of her life?

Joss's steps slowed until she turned to face Malone who stilled the mare she led with a silent command. "I'm not going to call it off. I can guess what was going to happen to me if I hadn't gotten away. But, Malone, I would've died first. I promise you. I would've killed or died or maybe both. Some girls aren't that strong. I think about those two younger girls, and I want to cry for them. I don't know where they are. If they even survived trying to get away. I want to hurt someone."

Malone caught her up and held her close. "I know, Joss. Me, too. We'll hurt them most by stopping them or at least hindering them as much as we can. But you're what's most important to me now. Just don't run, okay. No matter what. Promise me. Don't run."

"I promise."

Joss's voice was steady, and Malone drew a deep breath of relief. "Let's get this done, then."

They made quick work of unsaddling and brushing Jaz and making sure everyone had hay and a clean bucket of fresh water.

Cade and Ryder stepped from the shadows as she and Joss approached their trailer. When Malone would have made introductions, Cade shook his head and gestured toward the trailer door. As Malone made quick work of unlocking it, she realized her fingers were trembling slightly and hoped Joss didn't notice. That would do nothing to reassure the girl that all would be well.

Once inside, Malone felt suddenly chilled. Ryder accepted her offer to make coffee. Cade simply watched with a steady gaze as she readied the coffee pot.

She was glad when Ryder took the initiative, holding out his hand to Joss, waiting quietly until she shook hands with him.

"You're the U.S. Marshal."

"My name is James. James Ryder. I'm here to listen to your story. I can't fix what happened to you, but maybe I can prevent it from happening to someone else. Even one someone else. That's how I know I've made a difference."

At his words, Joss seemed to relax. Malone wondered

if, hoped that, the reason was at least partly because her trust was strong in Cade and Malone, herself.

Without rushing, yet without wasting time, Ryder opened the subject of Joss's abduction and escape.

"I want you to tell me everything you can remember, Joss, but I want you to start further back from when you woke up in that semi. I want you to start with the day you walked into your last foster home."

Malone tensed, but where once the girl would have dropped her chin to allow her hair to hide her features and her emotions, Joss lifted her chin. She started talking, telling her story in a low but strong voice. Malone hated hearing it again but, for Joss's sake, she kept her expression neutral, glad to busy herself with the coffee pot even for a little while.

"So, you don't recall your foster parents having visitors."

Joss looked surprised but only for a moment. "Sorry, I didn't mean to make you think that. They did, but always late, after I was in my room. At least he did. He had card games a couple of times a week. I know there was drinking and I could smell cigars and cigarettes, but I never saw anyone."

"What about voices? Did you hear anyone?"

"I could hear they were talking but not what they were saying. I'm sorry."

"No apology needed." Ryder's expression turned grim. "Except to you."

He listened intently as he walked Joss through waking up in the false bottom of a trailer, of her escape, and her worries for the other girls, her hopes that Ryder could find them.

When Joss finished, Ryder accepted a second cup of

coffee from Malone and began making notes in a small notebook. She offered one to Cade, but he shook his head. Instead, he tugged her down to sit beside him on the sleeper sofa Joss used. "She's doing fine."

"I know," she whispered, "but I'm not."

Cade pulled her in close, and she sighed as she allowed him that liberty. "Joanne looks good," she murmured.

"Yes, she does. But not as good as you," Cade said easily. He seemed to understand that Malone needed to tune out the sound of the conversation going on beside them. She needed to not think about what so easily could have been the fate of a young girl who'd come to mean so much to her. And, just maybe, she needed some reassurance that their meeting today wasn't a restart of an old relationship. "And," he added, "she still talks too fast and too damn much."

Malone laughed softly against his chest and felt, more than heard, his hum of pleasure at the sound. Malone liked the unexpected feeling that had her breath catching her in her throat. The timing sucked, but timing usually did.

"The good thing I got from all that chatter was that we aren't likely to lose our contract for use of the facility, despite two deaths in two days."

"You were afraid of that?"

"Everything about that deal has scared me. It was a risk moving from a place we've done business with for years, with a team who knows how to set up—not just for a rodeo—but for something as big as this. I had no idea what to expect in spite of all the assurances. But it's been good for the association, and Joanne says it's been good for the city. Apparently, she dogged out the local PD over their failure to keep everyone associated with us safe. This modernization means a lot to her."

His admission surprised her. It also reassured her as nothing else could have. He was no longer the autocratic, always right, young adult he'd been. He wasn't afraid to let her see his insecurities. That was real strength in a man.

A change in Ryder's tone as he asked Joss his next question pulled Malone back into the moment. "I need you to tell me about the truck, the trailer. Describe it to me as best you can."

Joss hesitated. "I'll try, but it was dark, and my head wasn't clear. And I was so scared. It wasn't like a horse trailer."

"Maybe a stock trailer? I've seen some here at the back of the arena."

"Not quite like those. It was a big truck kind of trailer. It was a long way down when I jumped onto the guy with the guns. But the sides were slatted, not solid. I've seen them on the highways, hauling little calves or crates of chickens. I haven't seen any here."

"Any kind of logo or name on the cab of the truck?"

"I didn't look. I just got up off the ground and ran." She looked disappointed in herself.

"You did exactly what you needed to do. You saved yourself. To have hesitated, even one split second to look around, could have cost you your life. Joss, I'll be honest. Chances are I'll never hear anything about the girls who were with you. I'll also tell you that could as easily be a good thing as a bad thing."

Ryder got to his feet, and Malone studied Joss anxiously before giving a sigh of relief. The girl looked less tense than at any point since the day she and the stowaway had faced each other down.

* * *

Cade didn't want to leave Malone, but he had no real reason to linger. It was late, and she and Joss looked exhausted.

He touched her cheek in a silent message and exited the trailer with Ryder. They walked a short distance and paused to talk quietly. "Did that help?" Cade knew it had been traumatic for Joss to share her story with a stranger. He didn't want it to have been in vain.

"Everything helps. I just don't always know how at the time," Ryder admitted. "I gather slivers of information however I can get them and put them together when I can. I'll find these bastards. I can promise you that much."

"And the foster parents."

Ryder's smile was somehow grim while genuine. "Now see, that's the best part. I get to nail those bastards for sure. And, with any luck, they'll spill their guts to lighten their sentences."

"I don't want their sentence lighter." Cade's hands were clenched into fists, and he knew what he wanted in place of that was a chance to pound the couple, both of them, into the ground.

"I'll do my dead level best to make sure it isn't—even if they come out feeling like it is at the time. And this could lead back to a real bust, something a hell of a lot bigger than this one couple. If it does, you getting Joss to talk to me could mean we put a lot of people in jail right along with them."

Cade shook his head. "I won't take credit. Joss wanted to talk to you, didn't want other foster kids put in that home. She's one brave girl."

"She'll have to be brave again when she tells her story to the judge in their case, but I'll push for that to happen soon. She's a minor and a victim. I suspect we can get that to happen in a closed session so she never has to see the bastards who sold her again."

As Ryder walked away, Cade snapped his fingers to bring Townsend to heel. A streak of gray nearly bowled the Aussie over, but the dog gave only a slight yip of surprise, and Cade recognized Callahan. He anticipated the swipe of a sheathed paw against his leg and the head-butting that warned he was expected to follow. And to be fast about it.

With Townsend at his side, he shadowed the cat closely, praying he wasn't destined to find another murder victim. They moved in near silence through the sometimes neat and sometimes scattered rows of now darkened trailers. The grounds were so quiet around them, he could hear the click of Townsend's toenails on the pavement. There wasn't a sound from the gray cat.

In less than ten minutes, the cat looked at him from the rail of a truck bed. Cade stepped closer. A security light cast enough glow for Cade to make note of a tire jack, a worn pair of boots, and a spur. He stared trying to make sense of what he saw, denying it even as he recognized the plain leather strap and the tracery of black inlay.

With a heavy heart, he turned to look at the trailer, forced himself to move, to knock on the trailer door. After a moment, he heard a stumbling inside, and then Luke peered out at him sleepily and a bit anxiously.

"Mr. Cade? Is something wrong?"

"I need to speak to your dad."

Luke looked even more anxious. "He's not here. I came

in while he was talking with Dawson White. I guess they went someplace together. Is everything okay?"

"Probably. Just something on my mind. Tell him I came by, okay?"

"Sure. Should I call him?"

"No." Cade had to force himself not to respond with alarm at the suggestion. "It's not that urgent. We can talk in the morning. Get some rest."

By the look on the boy's face, Cade didn't think that was likely to happen. He hoped the kid stayed inside and safe until he figured out what was going on. As much as he disliked the sight of that spur in Brax's truck, recognizing it as a match to the one he'd given Ryder, he disliked the thought of Brax in conversation with Dawson White even less. Things were about to get ugly.

His most urgent thought was to get back to Malone and Joss. There were now too many connections. Joss's abduction. Ryder's investigation. The deaths of two men. No way was all of this not connected. And somehow, Brax Roberts, a man he'd always considered a good role-model for kids learning to rope and ride, was caught up in all of it. Perhaps more than caught up, he might be front and center.

Dread filled him, and he and the cat sprinted side by side toward Malone's trailer.

It seemed to Malone she had barely locked the door behind Cade and the marshal when she was opening it again to Tyge's voice and the pounding of his fist on her door.

"What the hell, Tyge!" She had a moment's thought that she didn't need to be cursing in front of Joss who sat on the edge of the sleeper couch, watching warily.

"You've got to get out of here, Malone. You and the girl! You're both in danger."

Joss stood abruptly, and Malone glanced her way, seeing the fear in the girl's eyes, the scattering of light freckles, suddenly emphasized by a face leached of color.

Malone's gaze swept the fading bruises on Tyge's face. "What's happened now?"

"There's not any time for explanations. I've got to get you someplace safe."

"I don't know what's going on, but I'm not leaving, Tyge. I'll fight, I've got a gun and I'll fight, but I won't leave."

"Shit, Malone." Tyge grasped her arm lightly, and for a moment, she thought he might pull her from the trailer, then she heard a sickening thud, and Tyge was falling forward into her arms. She stared in shock at his back, at the hole in his shirt, the blood that welled instantly.

In that instant, she froze, realizing her danger. Framed in the open doorway with Tyge heavy in her arms, she was exposed to whoever held the gun. Looking up, she stared without understanding into the eyes of Brax Roberts. She thought he said 'I'm sorry' before he lifted the gun again but the words were lost to Joss's scream and a shot fired wildly as Brax fell beneath Cade's weight.

* * *

Cade suspected that, for the rest of his life, he'd never forget that heart-wrenching second of fear between seeing that gun aimed at Malone and finding the wits to launch himself at a man he would never have suspected of committing any crime, much less human trafficking and murder.

Even now, leaned against the trailer with Malone cradled against his chest, his arms wrapped around her, he couldn't slow the hard thuds of his heartbeat as they waited for the ambulance and Ryder to arrive. He doubted his pulse would ever return to normal.

Lying just inside the trailer door, Tyge was alert and cursing with pain. Cade suspected the bullet had hit a rib but, thank God, not his heart. The slow welling of blood was not the gush of heart or artery. As little fondness as Cade had for the cowboy, he didn't wish him dead, and he sure as hell didn't need another body on the grounds.

Brax sat with his hands tied with hay string, staring at the gun in Cade's hand. Every now and then Cade glanced at the cat who crouched with his ears pinned flat, a fierce yellow gaze on Brax. Beside him, Townsend growled each time the man so much as shifted positions. But Brax wasn't even trying to get away.

Joss stood close and quiet, holding Malone's hand.

When Ryder showed up, he looked from the gun in Cade's hand to the one lying close to Brax's feet. "He might've made you shoot him."

"He might have," Cade said quietly, and Ryder nodded. Cade added, "I didn't call Marchmann."

"Out of his league. He'll be mad as hell, but I'll take care of it. This one belongs to the feds." He paused. "I guess the cat helped you nail him."

Cade sighed. "I'm afraid so, and, no, I can't explain any better than that."

Ryder shook his head in amusement. "Any others to go along with him?"

"You'll want to look hard at Dawson White."

"I can help with that." It was the first time Brax had spoken since Cade had planted him on the pavement. One side of his face looked like he'd been drug across asphalt. Cade took great pleasure in that, but it was far less than he wanted to do to the man.

Cade felt Malone shift and reluctantly let her go. She walked over to Brax and looked down at him. "Why?" He heard the bewilderment in her voice. "You tried to kill Tyge. Then you aimed the gun at me, and you were going to pull the trigger. And Joss next? Why?"

Brax shook his head and looked away. Joss crossed to her and looked expressionlessly down at Brax before she turned her back on him and hugged Malone.

Cade wanted more than anything to stay with Malone but, now that she was safe, there was something else he had to do. Someone had to go tell Luke, and Cade knew that someone had to be him. And he dreaded it.

Unexpectedly, the boy gave some insight when Cade told him about his father's arrest. "I don't know the whole of it, Luke, but I know he was involved in some bad stuff."

Tears leaked from Luke's eyes. "My dad's not a bad man. If he did bad things, it's because of money. He thinks I don't know, but we still get bill after bill from when mama was sick. There wasn't any insurance, and the year after she died the drought hit us hard. We lost crops and calves and couldn't pay that year's mortgage on the farm. We caught up some last year…" His voice trailed and Cade suspected he realized the *catching up* had come at the expense of others, innocent others.

"I'm sorry, son." As much as he would've liked to agree with Luke that his dad wasn't a bad person, he couldn't say the reassuring words. "I've called your uncle. He's on his way to get you and take care of things here." Cade hadn't a clue if the man would try to post bond for Luke's dad. He didn't even know if a judge would set bail, considering the crimes committed. He doubted it. But that was for someone else to learn and share with the man's son. Cade wouldn't speculate.

What Cade could do was comfort a frightened and grieving young man, and he pulled Luke against his chest and let him cry.

Chapter 20

I suppose this rodeo life is perfect for those who love it, but it seems like way too much hard work to me. I subscribe to the theory work smarter not harder, and there doesn't seem to be much leeway with this sport. But it is exciting, I'll grant you that. Especially now, on this final day. I've determined that Malone is neck and neck in money earnings with two other contestants, and it all comes down to this final day, this final run for the money.

"Ladies and Gentlemen, our next rider is Malone Summers, a long-time professional in the sport of rodeo. Her fellow competitors know that Ms. Summers lost her beloved Jupiter to a tragic accident two years ago. Six months ago, after that heartbreak, just as they were clocking some of the best times on the circuit, Ms. Summer's good horse Casey was permanently sidelined with an injury. Some barrel racers only get one true champion barrel horse in a lifetime. Ms. Summers has had—or should I say created—many more than that. And now I'd like to introduce you to JJ's Red Jasmine, a rescue horse that has been rescued indeed. Ms. Summers calls her Jaz, and her hopes are riding high on the big red mare's ability."

Unexpectedly, I feel my own heart pounding with excitement. There must be something exhilarating about riding a very large horse through an intricate pattern of incredible speed, brief slow-downs, and what look to be sling-shot turns. There is also that twinge of fear for my temporary human who looks so small and fragile above the massive creature.

As they fly back toward the alleyway, the announcer, always so professional and in control, unexpectedly shouts with excitement as he calls out the time. Apparently, our girl has set a new record for the week. I'm happy for her. Malone's life hasn't always been easy, but I don't think she expects easy. She takes each day with a sense of joy, and Joss is beginning to do the same.

As for me? This case is closed, and I'm ready to find my way back to Dax. I'll need a little help with that, but I haven't a doubt that Malone will make it happen.

* * *

Malone slowed Jaz as they hit the alleyway. Her heart was so full, she wondered that it could hold all of her happiness in that moment. Jaz was everything she'd hoped and needed her to be. Never a replacement for Jupiter, never a replacement for Casey, but a treasure and a joy in her own right. Malone knew she was blessed to be able to make her living in just this way, and she never, ever took that or the animals that enabled her to do it for granted.

Midway down the alley, Cade stepped away from the

fence panel and placed a hand on Jaz's rein. Malone looked into his eyes, and it felt like coming home. For a moment, she was twelve to his seventeen, at the beginning of a crush that had turned into so much more and lasted a lifetime. For both of them.

* * *

I ride shotgun, looking out Cade's truck window, having switched vehicles at the last truck stop. There's too much girl talk going on in the other, which is fine if you're a female. But I understand new beginnings are exciting. Malone is moving herself, Joss, and her horses back home to LaGrange, Georgia which is close to Cade's family abode. No coincidence in all that, I suspect.

They've warned Frank and Kelli that they're swinging by the newlyweds' place to get me back with Dax.

The wrap up of this case has felt good. I enjoyed watching while the villains were arrested … I always like that part.

I can't help but believe it would be good for Joss to witness the arrest of the couple who sorely betrayed her, but maybe Malone is right. Joss is better off if spared any further sight of them. I wish she could be spared the memory of them, but Malone is certain time and love will heal all wounds.

As for me, I wish I could've been present when the foster parents were handcuffed and forced—dragged, I hope—from their home, but at least I was there when Joss was told they'd been captured and would never again harm an innocent person.

There was a bittersweet moment for Malone when Tyge was carried away on a stretcher in handcuffs. He saved her life, after all, and they once meant a lot to each other. Cade has since learned and shared that Tyge has a chance at probation or at least a lighter sentence. Tyge wisely spilled everything he knew to the authorities.

And I have a concession to make. The sight of the Aussie standing guard over Brax Andrews was unexpected and appreciated. He's earned the right to his dignity. Townie is no more. Townsend, it is.

Malone and Joss plan to turn the old homestead into a training facility for young equestrians who have a goal of becoming rodeo competitors. Not that she's planning to retire from competition, so they'll be busy. It's hard work, but I know Cade will bring energy and muscle to the task. I expect to hear wedding bells tinkling in the future.

For now, if Townsend will give me room on this seat, I need a nap.

* * *

Malone braked at the entrance to Frank and Kelli's place and stepped down from the truck. Behind her, Cade did the same, and Callahan followed him with a leap.

The young man at the gate had clearly been waiting, but he didn't look impatient. He lifted a hand in greeting then watched as Callahan turned in front of Malone and stared up at her. She bent, gathering the cat to her, rubbing her face against his now-familiar plush coat. Joss stepped out on her side of the truck and circled the hood for her turn at goodbye.

Morning sun glinted in the corner of the girl's eyes as she cradled the cat. It could be tears, Malone thought. Like her own. They'd never forget him.

Reluctantly Joss placed Callahan at her feet and reached for Malone's hand. Together they watched as the cat twined around Cade's legs. Cade crouched to run his hand along the cat's back. Callahan gave the cowboy an intense look, then turned to bump Townsend with his head before he walked to Dax and rubbed against well-worn army boots.

Dax bent low and Callahan climbed onto his backpack. With another wave and a nod from the man, the duo started down the road. Malone had no doubt Callahan would soon find himself embroiled in another adventure, another someone who needed his help, another mystery that needed solved. He was that kind of cat.

Thank you for taking the time to read *Callahan Goes Rodeo*. If you enjoyed it, please consider telling your friends or posting a short review. Word of mouth is an author's best friend and is much appreciated.
Thank you!
Susan

* * *

Susan Yawn Tanner is a bestselling author in the romance and mystery genres. When she isn't writing, she's either tending her horses or barrel racing. Although she lives less than an hour from the Gulf of Mexico, the white sandy beaches of Mississippi can't compete with the lure of arena dirt.

Sign up for Susan's newsletter where she announces new books and exciting giveaways.
susanytanner.com

www.ingramcontent.com/pod-product-compliance
Lightning Source LLC
Chambersburg PA
CBHW030422120726
47903CB00003B/766